THE
DREAMGIVERS

G·K
Hall
&Co.

THE DREAMGIVERS

Jim Walker

G.K. Hall & Co.
Thorndike, Maine

Published in 1997 by arrangement with Bethany House Publishers.

G.K. Hall Large Print Western Collection.

The text of this Large Print edition is unabridged.
Other aspects of the book may vary from the original edition.

Set in 16 pt. Plantin by Al Chase.

Printed in the United States on permanent paper.

Library of Congress Cataloging in Publication Data

Walker, James, 1948–
    The dreamgivers / Jim Walker.
        p.   cm.
    ISBN 0-7838-1997-8 (lg. print : hc)
    1. Frontier and pioneer life — West (U.S.) — Fiction.   2. Large
type books.   I. Title.
    [PS3573.A425334D74   1997]
    813'.54—dc20   96-43692

To Joel
A man I greatly admire,
my friend, and my son.

The Wells Fargo Trail

Book I

CHAPTER 1

The body lay face down in the shallows. From the edge of the road, the men watched the surge of the tide begin to move it out to sea.

"I'll get him. Fetch me a rope from the back of the buggy and bring it, pronto." Zac Cobb slipped off his gun belt and let it drop to the floor of the buckboard. His boots dug into the soft sand. Stopping in his tracks, he wrenched them off, and then continued his sprint toward the water. A skittering crowd of sandpipers retreated in all directions as he ran past them.

Without looking back, he plunged into the icy water, diving headfirst under the oncoming waves. Breaking the surface, he blinked back the salt water from his eyes and tossed his head, straining to see. He could feel the pull of the tide and the strong current and knew that if it was moving him out to sea, it was also towing the man he and Talbot had sighted from the beach. Unable to spot the floating body, but assuming it was hidden by the swells, Zac began to swim toward open water to get into position to intercept it. He knew he had to hurry before the cold water had its effect.

There he was! Zac gyrated toward the rising swell and submerged. Surfacing, he swam in the direction of the drifting man. With several powerful kicks, he drew closer and, reaching out, grabbed the man's ankle and swung him around. The lifeless body was dressed in black silk clothing. Straining against the tide, Zac began to slowly tow it back to shore.

"Zac! Zac! I found the line." Race Talbot, a longboat whaler, had shaped a loop and was spinning it over his head. Wading into the surf, he stood in front of the shore break and shouted over the breakers, "I'll get it to you! The surf is pretty strong and that current will take you out." He took a few more steps and hollered, "Swim parallel to the beach, try to get closer and I'll get this to you."

Zac turned the body over and placed his arm around the man. He didn't take the time to look over the remains, but he noticed the pigtail. The man's black hair had been laced tightly and knotted into a row. Zac drew him closer to get better control. Most white people wouldn't even come close to a Chinaman, but now Zac was risking his neck to recover a cadaver. He didn't even think about it, he just pulled harder, gulping brine with every wave.

It was laborious to swim against the tide with only one arm, but soon he saw Race spinning the loop off to his right. The line uncurled in the air and dropped smoothly across his path. He hooked the coil around his lifeless companion's head and shoulder and then swam straight for the shore.

Zac crawled out of the surf and collapsed, exhausted and chilled to the bone, on the warm, wet sand. After a moment, he looked up to see Talbot pulling the body into the shore break, and watched as the silk-covered foreigner coasted onto the beach. Talbot used his might to pull the body still farther onto the wet sand, and Zac got up to take a closer look.

"Looky here, Zac. This feller didn't drown, now that's for sure." Talbot suddenly stood up and walked away from the body, staring up the beach.

Bending down, Zac studied the corpse. The single gunshot wound to the man's chest cavity and a large area of powder burns caught his attention first. He lifted the man's small frame from the sand and saw the size of the exit wound. Zac could see that the murder weapon had been a large caliber gun fired at close range.

Leveling the body back down on the sand, Zac lifted the man's arm. He could tell by the subtlety of movement in the limb that the man hadn't been dead long. Whoever had done this was still close by.

He looked up to see Talbot still staring in the opposite direction. "You know this man, Race?"

"No, sir, can't 'zackly say I do."

"Well, this whale oil of yours is going to a Chinese market in San Luis, isn't it?"

"True enough, but that don't mean I know this feller." Talbot turned to face Cobb, who was still stooped over the dead man. " 'Sides, him being

9

Chinese and all, I might have seen him a hundred times and still couldn't say for sure. For the life of me, I don't know how they tell each other apart."

"Well, let's get him into town. Maybe one of those customers of yours will recognize him."

The two men carried the corpse to the wagon. They then strapped some oat bags on, for the mules to feed, and sat down in the sun to dry off and eat their lunch.

Zac watched a snow-white crane gliding toward the beach near some trees farther along the road. Unexpectedly, it swerved from its graceful path and flew away. A twinkle of distant sunlight from the same stand of trees brought the hair on the back of Zac's neck to attention.

Memories of Virginia — recollections of three years spent watching the reflections of brass buttons, gun barrels, and binoculars — made him instantly wary of the sudden flash of light. Squinting, he pulled his gray felt hat lower to block out the glare of the sunlight on the water and studied the tree line for movement.

"Put your lunch up, Race, I think we got company."

The long-boater stopped chewing and his jaw dropped open.

"Is there something you're not telling me, Talbot?"

The whaler gulped, then quickly shook his head.

Zac always made it a point to be more prepared

than any opposition he might face. He knew the whaling season had finished and the road was well-traveled by dead-broke seamen. Instinctively, he unfastened the leather thong on his Peacemaker's hammer. Since the apprehension of bandits for Wells Fargo was his stock-in-trade, he was not about to become a victim of one. He kept this part of his life quietly concealed in town while maintaining his own life as a rancher, biding his time until the company called.

He put what remained of the sandwich his old German cook, Hans, had packed for him back into the leather bag and, deciding not to light his pipe, he reached under the seat for the flour sack he carried. Through the rough material, he felt for the hammers of his sawed-off Meteor ten-gauge and cocked both barrels. At close quarters this was the ultimate equalizer. It always had the final say. He'd heard the old saying, "Buckshot means burying," and believed it to be true.

He looked at Talbot and noted the fear that appeared in the man's eyes when he heard the two hammers cock under the cloth. "Pays to be prepared," he said. Laying the hand howitzer on the seat with the muzzle pointed away, he eased the buckboard back to the sandy trail and slapped the reins.

Minutes later, he saw three men walk out from the trees that hugged the shoreline. He didn't recognize them, but he saw the strangers for what they were, sailors on the uncertain deck of dry land.

He slowed and walked the team cautiously forward as the men stepped out into the bright sun. A man with a red beard carried the looking glass in one hand and a Barns .50 caliber boot pistol suspended around his neck and shoulder by a rope lanyard. It looked to be just the sort of weapon that could have made the hole in the man they had just saved from the fish. The other two black-bearded men carried Colt Navies tucked behind wide leather belts.

Zac swung the buckboard to the left to try to put the mules out of harm's way, giving him a free field of fire to his right, should it become necessary. The tense black-bearded men in their pea coats raked their eyes over the two of them sitting stone still in the buckboard, their careful glances taking note of Zac's Colt with the thong lifted from the hammer. Talbot, Zac had noticed earlier in the day, had been carrying a sidearm. Now the weapon was hidden under his tightly buttoned coat.

"Goot morning to ye, goot sirs," the redbeard spouted in a booming brogue. "Might me mates and I be having a lift into that fine town up ahead?"

Talbot nervously turned his head to Zac, and in a barely audible tone said, "Let's just drive on." Ignoring him, Zac silently continued to look the strangers over, his agate-colored eyes measuring every inch of the men, evaluating every twitch and each nervous glance. For him, confrontation was a living science, the discipline of

12

staying alive. Not that he enjoyed confrontation, but he was always ready for it. He dropped his chin, using the brim of his hat to shield his eyes.

"Don't know if you boys will want to ride with us. We got the body of a man we fished out of the bay riding back there. Might make the travel a bit disagreeable for y'all." He noticed that none of the men seemed surprised by the announcement, nor the least bit curious as to the identity of the corpse.

The red-bearded sailor smiled. "Oh, don't pay us no mind. We're seamen who've been accustomed to many a dying in our time."

Zac jerked his thumb pointing to the back of the buggy. "You fellas can get in the back, but the sidearms will have to ride up front with me."

The redbeard quickly doffed his crushed black mate's cap, exposing a healthy shock of uncut, flaming hair. He twisted the hat in his hands and slowly swung his head from side to side, taking careful aim into the eyes of his companions.

"Well now, sir, as ye can see we 'err simple seamen. We mean ye no harm. We be just put about to see the sights in your fine land before sailing off to the Far East. We're just a wee bit curious about news of the gold strike in those Sierras of yours as well. You gentlemen wouldn't want to leave us adrift and defenseless, now, would ye?"

Zac had seen many sailors on the coast, yet couldn't remember any armed with anything more lethal than a splicing knife. Firearms just weren't the normal tools of a seaman's trade. It was what had made Talbot's sidearm all the more noticeable when they started out that morning from Cambria.

"Somehow, gentlemen, defenseless isn't quite the word one would use to describe you boys. Now, I'm not a nervous man, but that's because I'm a careful one. I do my best to fight shy of trouble and I'd advise you boys to do the same. Take your choice, ride with me minus your sidearms, or walk."

It was plain to see that the discussion was over from Zac's perspective. He reached down to grab hold on the reins. Instantly, the pea-coated sailors fastened their hands onto the grips of their revolvers. One of the pistoleers pulled his clear and, stepping to the front of the pack, aimed it directly at Zac and shook the barrel.

"All right, farmer, you listen here. Make one move for that six-gun, and just as surely as you sit there," — the man's gun barrel waggled at Zac — "I'll send you straight to hell. Make no mistake about it."

The redbeard placed a hand on his companion's arm and tried to calm him. Then, replacing his cap, he cocked it to the side of his head and planted his hands on his hips.

"Now, goot sirs," he said, "no cause for great alarm. Simple sailors such as ourselves have no desire for spilt blood. We fancy to be tidy about this whole business, we do." He pointed toward the team. "We'll take your steeds and this extra fine rig they are a pulling and go our own way. We just want what you're carrying."

"Just give 'em what they want," Talbot said.

Zac ignored the unsolicited advice and looked at the redbeard. "Why would you want what I've got back there?" He carefully placed the reins on the bottom of the buckboard. "Take my advice, there's lots easier ways to get to the Sierras than by mules." He paused and gazed for a long moment at the drawn, brandished revolver, then refocused on the red-haired sailor.

"Don't mistake me for just a sod-buster. If I wanted to, I could have drilled this man of yours before he had that horse pistol pulled. Now, my offer's still open. You can have a ride to town or a trip to Potter's Field, but those are the only two cards in the deck."

"Enough of this talk." The sailor with the drawn revolver cocked the hammer and stepped toward the buggy. "You two get down from there. We're taking what you've got."

Zac reached over and picked up the sack. He pointed the burlap bag toward the sailor with the outstretched revolver. "Well, don't forget to take this," he held out the sack. "Right now it's the most valuable thing I've got."

Without blinking an eye, he squeezed off both triggers, knowing the shock power the two together carried might mean the other men would cut and run. Besides, he figured the fella with the bony finger and the hell-bound threat was asking for the whole hog.

The explosion roared through the air and sent smoke, lead, burlap, and terror in all directions. It stung Zac's hand, whipped the mule's ears into a panic, and catapulted the pea-coated sailor several feet into the air and onto the ground. The wadding was still sizzling in the man's-jacket as he lay, suddenly very still.

Talbot jumped to the ground, putting the rig between him and the sailors.

His hand stinging from the blast, Zac dropped the half-wrapped shotgun to the bottom of the buckboard and extracted his Shopkeeper .45. The smoke and terror that shook the other two bandits had momentarily taken their wits away and caused their eyes to bulge at the frightful sight of their dead partner.

The surviving black-coated sailor stumbled backward as he drew his revolver, knocking his hat off in the wild confusion and exposing a bald pate that, from Zac's point of view, made an excellent target. Still stumbling backward, the man began to point, cock, and shoot in terrible confusion and with rapid succession. Meanwhile, the redbeard had slid his hand down the lanyard, palming the grip on his Barns. He found the sight, lifted the long boot pistol, and extended his arm to shoot.

Zac looked at the bald-headed sailor through the notch on the cocked hammer and fired off a round. Combat shooting was an occupational study for Zac. He handloaded his own ammunition and made sure that the shopkeeper belly gun

16

he carried came with loads of half powder and half cornstarch. The reduced recoil in this special load of his allowed him to get off a better targeted second shot. Besides, he didn't want his slug passing through his target. He wanted it to rattle around and stay in the machinery where it could do some damage. In his years with the company, Zac had become a rather dispassionate hunter of men.

He felt cold and distant inside. His indifference with dispensing death bothered him enormously, but in times like this, he knew the coldness served him well. It enabled him to mechanically go through the procedures of combat while facing death and danger. He'd worry about it later.

Gazing down the barrel for his second shot, he squeezed from the palm, milking the trigger. The first round had been off, but he sighted his second and more careful one into the gleaming and bobbing bald head. It landed with devastating impact about mid-forehead and dropped the pistol-wheeling sailor where he stood.

Zac had focused his attention on what appeared to be the more dangerous man, the one with the revolver. Suddenly, he felt the whir of the heavy lead ball from the boot pistol.

The denim collar around his neck ripped away from his shirt and searing fire burned the side of his throat. Looking away from the dead sailor, he saw the redbeard running away with pistol spent, no more bullets and no more fight. Zac placed his fingers on the painful sting and, glancing down, saw a streak of blood.

He looked back toward the fleeing robber, then extended his arm and steadied his aim down the barrel. Framing his forward sight on the back of the running man, Zac prepared to squeeze.

No, he thought, *I won't do it*. He cocked the hammer with his thumb and rested it back on the chamber, watching the fleeing seaman disappear into the trees. Placing his hand back on the side of his blistered neck, he knew how close he'd come.

He leaned over and saw Talbot sitting by the wheel, gun drawn but unfired. "You know, Race, if you're goin' to carry one of those things, you better be prepared to use it. You might confuse someone into shootin' you out of self-defense."

"Dang it, Cobb. You're some kinda hell on wheels. Where'd you learn how to do that? I ain't never seen the like."

Zac climbed down from the buggy. "From where you are, Talbot, you didn't see it this time, either."

Going through the dead men's pockets, Zac made a careful stash in his handkerchief of their possibles: sixty dollars in gold coins, one gold watch, three wedding bands, a railway baggage receipt, and a gold locket. It was doubtful any of the items belonged to the dead sailors, but he didn't look for any inscriptions on the wedding bands nor open the locket, figuring that would be the sheriff's business.

Sheriff Jeff Bridger was a nephew of Jim

Bridger, a frontiersman who had blazed the trail to the West. When the railroad came west, Jeff had taken his turn eliminating the buffalo. He fed the gandy dancers of the Central Pacific until he couldn't stand the mass killing any longer. The sickness of the smell finally drove him as far west as he could go without putting to sea.

He'd been to the gold fields, tried digging the dirt, then had to turn to prizefighting to make a living. A chest the size of a barrel sported the star that showed he was now sheriff of San Luis Obispo County, but he had a look in his sky-blue eyes that would have said "Lawman" even if a body couldn't see the star he was wearing.

Talbot took the buckboard to the undertaker and from there was going to make his delivery to the Chinese market. Zac pushed into Bridger's dimly lit office and dropped the sailors' handguns and the bulging handkerchief on the desk. "Jefferson, sorry to make work for you."

The sheriff raised his eyes and showed his teeth through a drooping blond mustache. It wasn't a smile, however, but a grimace. He folded his massive arms.

Zac nodded toward the newly delivered burden on the desk. "What you see there is what remains of a pair of seagoin' corpses Talbot and I met up with on the road from Cambria. They had ambitions on bein' highwaymen, but now their principal concern is burial."

"You ever see these men before?" Bridger asked. Zac slowly swung his head in the negative and pulled out his dark briarwood pipe. Bridger continued to probe, "I suppose they just sized you up as the gentleman farmer you pretend to be and decided to make you their pigeon."

The dark-eyed man fished in his duster for pipe tobacco, but made no response. Bridger could occasionally grow frustrated at his friend's constant difficulty in normal conversation, and Jeff Bridger was never anyone to let a thought between friends go unspoken. "Friend, you beat all."

Zac raised his eyebrows and checked the time on the gold watch that hung from his vest. "I know I ask a lot of you, Jeff. But you know I'd prefer to keep what I do as quiet as possible around here."

"Speaking of what you pretend to be, a telegram came in for you today. I was going to try to get it to you tomorrow, but you beat me to it."

Zac picked up the telegram. Turning it over, he noted that it originated from Visalia. Quickly, he stuck it in his pocket.

The sheriff methodically handled the revolvers. He sniffed each cylinder, checking the loads and pulling the remaining percussion caps. He cast a frozen stare at Zac and the telegram sticking out of the agent's pocket. "Been my observation they normally don't send for you unless they've got a long-term problem to deal with. Guess they know you're not the easiest man to reach."

Bridger opened the handkerchief and looked over the items as he laid them out on the smeared cotton cloth. "Oh, you can be reached all right," he went on, "but a body has to endure Francisco's palaver and that old German's cooking before he can get back home." Bridger removed paper from his desk drawer and dabbed his quill into the inkwell. "I need a detailed account of everything that happened." There was a pause. "You know, Cobb, I get powerfully tired of trying to drag thinking out of you. The wheels are turning up there in your head. I can see them move. Just likely as not though, nothing comes out."

"Well, Jeff, I guess some men are just more private."

"I'd say today, you've been pretty public at making trouble." He paused, then cracked a smile. "I guess I can't complain about this business today. Tarnation, I'm all-fired glad it was you those fellers decided on. I'm fearful to think of what would have took place if one of our ranchers' wives was in here bawling 'cause them boys laid out her husband."

Bridger removed paper from his desk drawer and dabbed his quill into the inkwell. "I need a detailed account of everything that happened. You know," — he looked up at Zac — "you keep drawing down and killing bandits two at a time, and you'll be getting yourself a label as a gunfighter. You'll become a known man, too quick to talk about."

"Weren't two of them," Zac said. "There were three. The third one, a redhead with a full beard, got clean away. We brought in three bodies though. The other one's a Chinaman I fished out of the water earlier. From the looks of the gunshot wound in him, I'd say the redbeard I let run shot him. Can't say for sure, just the size of the hole looks to be .50 caliber or better, and that's what the redhead was carryin'. Undertaker probably won't let Race bring the fella in though. When it comes to Chinese, you know how particular the dead are about who they sleep with around here."

"How'd you let one get away, Cobb? I never knew you to not be thorough."

"I had him in my sights, but I just couldn't bring myself to pull the trigger on a man runnin' away. Any man who kills when there's somethin' else he can do is a hotheaded fool in the makin'." Zac paused, then placed his hand on his blistered throat. "I let him run, but a half inch to the left and he'd a took my scrawny neck off."

Zac slapped the pipe into the palm of his hand to force out any old leavings from his last smoke. He blew into the end of the curled stem and then palmed it. "I'm no gunfighter. Never even held a pistol till I rode with Moseby, though I was taught how to shoot one with slow and careful deliberation by one of the best."

Bridger laced his fingers together and leaned his chair back against the wall, taking a little pride that he had goaded his friend into talking. "Who schools anybody to shoot without teaching them to do it with some partialness to haste?"

Zac loaded the briar pipe with dark, whiskey-soaked tobacco. "Captain Holms. He'd been a duelist in New Orleans. Probably killed more southerners down there by the canal before 1861 than Yankees after. The rules in duelin', I guess, were that you had only one shot, and you better have the courage to face hot lead comin' at you while you took the time to aim straight. If you couldn't do that, you shouldn't get yourself into harm's way in the first place. I guess I've kept that as my style."

Bridger smiled. "You are definitely acquainted with civilized killing, Cobb. This is the West, though, not the genteel South. The rule here is, there ain't no rules."

Zac struck a match on the end of his thumbnail and held it to the bowl of the pipe. He looked up at Bridger through the flame and the billowing smoke. "I write up my own by-laws of survival as I go along," he said. Drawing a long sip on the stem of his curled black pipe, he released dark blue smoke. "Still, a man has to know his strengths and I'm no speed merchant."

Bridger brought his chair forward with a thud. "Well, you may not be a gunfighter, Cobb, but you are most undeniably a cool-headed shootist." He pointed to the telegram sticking out of the agent's pocket. "Maybe whoever those orders take you to will play by your" — he paused for effect — " 'by-laws,' was it? Well, for your sake, I hope so." Bridger's radiant blue eyes flashed and sparkled. "Chasing after people with the company's gold can be bad for your health."

CHAPTER 2

Zac spent the night where he always wound up when he was in town. Before dawn, the back door to Ma Bowers' boardinghouse screeched open and a pan of night water swished past Zac's window. The chickens that went scurrying and squawking across the back of the yard to escape the water served as a rude wake-up call. Zac never got used to sleeping in a town. It was too hard to tell when the sun was coming up or going down.

"Get away from that door. You'll get yours in due time." Mrs. Bowers' voice was not exactly the one he wanted to wake up to, but she'd have to do this morning. Her sheets were the cleanest in town and her boardinghouse was away from the bawdy part of town, not proper nor possible to sleep in.

Zac rolled his rifle and shotgun into the bedroll and stuffed extra socks and a fresh-washed shirt into the cracks. Before heading out the back door, he deposited the company telegram into the hot potbellied stove. Taking a biscuit off the griddle, he laid his two dollars for the bed on the table. He swung his saddle onto one shoulder and called out to the old lady, "Much obliged for the bed and the biscuit." Tipping his hat, he excused himself from breakfast. "I'd stay for the eggs, but I've got a little social call to pay."

The gray-haired woman was dipping her hand into a pail of corn and scattering it to the chickens. "Zachary Taylor Cobb, you marry that girl," she said. "Why you'd want to live out there with a Mexican, that old German cook, and jes' yourself is beyond the sense of any normal human being." Zac nodded in a way that showed he was listening and thinking. He knew Mrs. Bowers was just a mother who meddled. Her children had grown and gone, and so each guest appeased her gentle, henpecking nature.

He scurried out into the alley, lost in his own thoughts and meandering empty hopes about a morning with Jenny. *Jenny's a good friend,* he told himself, *but her blue eyes and blond curls make her someone hard to keep as only a friend.* Two years earlier, he was drawn to her at first sight, but something inside him refused to let it go any further. He knew there were mutual feelings on her part, but that only frightened him all the more.

Zac had told himself the risk of what he did ought to make him fight shy of marriage and a family. He couldn't afford a distraction. He was good at his job and his clear mind had saved his bacon many times. He knew intuitively that going out on an assignment and cluttering his thoughts with self-preservation at any price would get his ticket punched for sure. The fastest way to get killed was to duck at the wrong time.

He figured the thought of someone waiting at home was certain to creep into his brain at the wrong moment. It would take the edge off of everything that made him do what he did well. In his mind, he played and replayed his need for isolation. He knew the more he rehearsed the thinking the deeper his resolve would be when he saw her smile. Going to see her again wouldn't make it any easier, but he wasn't able to resist the feelings inside of him when he sat across the table from her. She had become dangerously special to him and hard to pull out of his soul. He even felt a mite protective.

Jenny had shown up in San Luis Obispo after the death of her fiance, the captain of the merchantman *Blue Swan*. When her man's ship went down, on its way back from the Far East, she left San Francisco to make new memories. What was to be a move to a cousin's in Los Angeles, however, only went as far as San Luis.

A stretch of the legs during a stagecoach ride made her fall in love with the sleepy little mission town. The same impulsiveness that had brought her west to marry the captain made her stay in San Luis. There wasn't much a single, decent woman could do, but Jenny had spunk and could make doughnuts and pies. She had an even better head for business, and in no time at all, she had a gold mine coming out of a secondhand stove in a rented storefront, a place she now owned.

As Zac's long strides took him quickly through the town, he noted the stark changes San Luis was undergoing with the approach of the railroad. The mission of Father Sierra and the sleepy stage stop that had grown up around it was becoming a boomtown. Oh, it wasn't one of those "Hell on Wheels" places he'd seen near other rail lines; Bridger would see to that. It was a different place though, all the same.

For one thing, a bubbling, steaming, caterwauling, back-alley culture of foreigners had sprung up. Overnight, shanty houses had appeared on the backside of town. Now, Chinese men stood in doorways smoking long-stemmed pipes and glaring at him as he wound his way to the cafe's back door. Women stirred boiling pots of laundry while screeching at their pig-tailed children. He looked into their eyes as he passed, inwardly searching for someone in grief, someone who might be connected to the man he'd pulled from the bay.

He walked around the building and deposited his load on the sidewalk outside the front window before entering the cafe. He found an empty chair and slipped his feet and bedroll under a table covered with a cheerful checkered cloth. Jenny saw him at once, and her eyes brightened as she pushed her hair back. She carried the coffeepot to his table and began to pour. "Zachary, I heard you were in town. Thought you might stop by."

"Well, I'd a been by a little earlier," he said, "but I had some freight to deliver and a telegraph to send off." Her shoulders slumped. She knew the telegram could only involve Wells Fargo. She knew all too well about his "other" occupation and treated it with cold silence.

"We have some fresh eggs this morning," she said.

Zac grinned. "Okay, if you'll vouch for them. I'll take some with a steak, if you've got one."

"My pleasure," she said. She started to leave the table, then paused and turned back to Zac. "I suppose you'll be needing some travel grub." Her eyes looked straight into his, hoping what she knew to be true was wrong.

Zac softened his smile and showed some of his southern charm. "Yes, I'll need some keepables, but what I'd prefer most is your breakfast company."

Jenny smiled coyly. "I believe I can arrange that," she said. "I have a new waitress helper; name's Me Che. She's one of the foreigners, but she can speak some American."

The little Chinese girl exploded through the kitchen doors. She balanced plates, food, and hot coffee while passing around the steaming array to a table full of local businessmen in the far corner. Jenny watched the girl and gave Zac a smile. "It's been hard for some of the local hardheads to take their food from a foreigner, but she's been a godsend for me."

After Jenny brought out his hot breakfast, Zac ate while she talked. One-sided conversation with Zac never bothered Jenny like it did Bridger. She read answers into the way he smiled, and had learned to interpret his thoughts even when they weren't spoken. Zac said much, even when saying nothing.

Toward the end of their breakfast, Zac noticed a seafarer slide through the front door. The new-comer ambled over to the group of businessmen holding court in the corner and took a seat.

The men had finished their meals and were talking and smoking cigars with their coffee. A red-headed Irishman with loud laughter and a booming brogue rose to slap the back of the new-comer.

Zac studied the redhead carefully. Although he noted the similarities to the man he had allowed to escape on the road the day before, he knew he wasn't looking at the same person. The new-comer looked over to Zac's table and their eyes met briefly. Zac continued sawing on his steak, but he could tell that the sailor was continuing a steady stream of glances in Jenny's direction.

Noticing Zac's distraction, Jenny swung her head around and spotted the seaman. She nodded politely at the man, then turned back to Zac. "That's Captain Michael Hogan. He's the master of the merchantman *Blue Goose*. He knew my fiance. I should go over and say something to him. Would you like me to introduce you?"

Zac sipped his coffee. "No, I think I've had my fill of sailors for a while. I'll just sit right here and drink my coffee."

"You'd like him," she said. "He's traveled all over the world."

Zac pushed out his bottom lip and took his

29

pipe from his pocket.

Jenny could see her attempt to socialize him would get nowhere. "Oh, all right, Zac Cobb. You never were much for groups anyway. When you take that pipe out, it means you've made up your mind and you don't want to talk about it."

"Jen, my druthers are just to set a spell. You go ahead on."

"Suit yourself. Just stay here and smoke your pipe. I'll be right back."

As she walked over to where the men were seated, the captain rose to his feet and extended his hand. Zac lit his pipe, making a disinterested study of the distant conversation. When Jenny turned to leave, the dark-bearded sailor put a hand on her shoulder. He stepped aside from the table, took something out of his pocket, and pressed it into her hand. In Zac's mind, minutes appeared to pass as the man stood talking intently to her. The captain looked into her eyes and held her hand as he folded her fingers over his offering.

Zachary's independence suddenly made him feel uncomfortable. The smug glimpse the captain cast over Jenny's shoulder as she turned to walk back to Zac's table caused the blood to rise to the back of his neck and stiffened his spine. The captain's glance in his direction was a look of knowing appraisal, one designed to make Zac feel small.

Jenny dropped what the man had given her into her apron pocket and, signaling to the Chinese girl, walked back and stood in front of Zac.

"Please excuse me for only a minute more. I promise I'll be back before your coffee gets cold."

Me Che came to her side. After whispering instructions to the girl, Jenny stepped out the front door. There, she began to talk to a seaman in a white shirt. Zac could see the dark-skinned man jump to his feet when she put her hand on his shoulder. He was short in stature but broadly built around the shoulders and chest. His thick, well-muscled legs stuck out several inches below the bottom of his tattered trousers. Propping one bare foot halfway up his other leg, the man stood balancing himself. Standing that way, Zac thought the man looked like a stork sporting the frame of a baby bull.

Me Che came from the kitchen and went out the front door with a plate of doughnuts and a glass of milk. Smiling broadly, Jenny took the offerings and handed them to the man, who now stood on two legs. He bowed repeatedly to her, smiling with a grin that exposed large white teeth. Zac noticed that Jenny patted the shoulder of the grinning stranger and returned his bow before she came back into the cafe and hurried to his table, where the remains of Zac's breakfast were growing cold.

"I'm sorry," she said. "That was Tiataglo. He's a harpooner that Captain Hogan found in the South Seas. He's intensely loyal to the captain. He travels into town with him but never wants to come inside. He doesn't feel people would approve of a dark skin in the cafe." She shook her head.

"I've told him I don't care what they think. Heaven knows I've taken enough grief for hiring a Celestial waitress. Still . . ." Jenny paused before continuing, "he insists on staying outside." Her long face perked up at a thought and her eyes twinkled. She playfully lowered her voice and whispered, "He comes from a tribe of cannibals, but we've discovered" — she leaned forward and smiled — "he prefers doughnuts."

Zac laughed. He knew Jenny took great pleasure in making him laugh. "What brings a whaler here?" he asked. "Most of the whales are taken by longboats from these shores. Hardly any room for merchantmen off this coast either. No major shipping point from San Luis."

"Well, the captain talks about important cargo out of China," she said.

Zac puffed on his pipe. "The only important cargo out of China these days is semi-slave labor for the railroads, and that's illegal now."

He cast a glance at the sailor sitting with the table full of men. "Of course, that would explain your friend's choice of his breakfast company." Zac puffed on the aromatic mix. "That railroad is supposed to bring us prosperity, but as near as I can figure, we're the ones bringing the prosperity to it."

Jenny smiled. "Now, if I didn't know better, I'd say that sounds a bit like jealousy, Mr. Cobb." Jenny's smile disappeared and she reached out and took hold of his left hand. "You know I fret about you when you go on one of these trips. I know times are hard, but I'm sure when the railroad comes in, things will change."

Zac had let the pipe go out. He pulled his hand out from under Jenny's and struck a match to relight the bowl. "Jen, the railroad will be good for you and the other merchants in town. Lord knows it'll bring some civilized changes hereabouts. For me, though, the changes won't be so good. When I got here, I bought my land for fifty cents an acre. Now, it's selling for ten times that amount, if it can be had at all. With the big ranches, the steel wire, and the type of money it takes to ship to market, I'll have to grow or die."

He drew deeply on the briar pipe and moved his face aside to keep the smoke out of Jenny's. "This Wells Fargo job can't go on forever. Doors are closing and I need all the reward money I can get to plow back into that spread."

"Don't take any unnecessary chances," Jenny said. She reached out and lightly touched Zac's hand as her plaintive blue eyes softly whispered an unspoken promise between the two of them. Zac knew that look. He also knew it came from a woman who had already spent too much time waiting for a man who didn't return. He knew that was an experience she hoped to never repeat. In a small way, he thought he was doing her a favor by trying not to get too close to her. At least, that was what he told himself.

He was a moth who had the best of reasons to

fly away from the flame: his job and his way of life. He could face the fear in his own heart, but the feeling of responsibility danger produced — that was different. It was something he was sure could cloud his better judgment at just the wrong time. He'd seen enough hardships of the innocent. No, he wasn't afraid of dying, but sometimes he wondered if he was afraid of living.

The war and his long walk through the smoldering South when it ended had shown Zac enough defenseless widows and their fatherless children. He'd been only a teenager himself during that shameful march home, a child with a gun. Every time he'd looked into one of those lonely, brokenhearted faces, he saw a piece of himself — the pain, the disappointment, the despair. He didn't want to see a widow or an orphan ever again, and he didn't want the everlasting shame of making one.

Something deep inside him also told him that to be responsible for someone was to be remembered for the empty space you left in their life after you were gone. It reminded him of how he felt even now — alone, an orphan of the war — and he didn't want to feel like one.

"All aboard! Everybody get on board if you're going!"

The call of the stage driver from the street snapped Zac's mind back to the present and broke his icy stare into Jenny's eyes.

"Visalia Stage, leaving in five minutes."

He tapped out his pipe. "Shorty won't wait."

He paused for another look into her eyes. "Don't get yourself het up," he said, "I'll come back."

"See that you do, Zachary Cobb." Her eyes brightened with humor and that familiar smile she frequently used. "You've run up quite a tab here and I wouldn't want to try to collect it from that cantankerous cook of yours."

Zac laughed. To smile and to hurt is to hurt less. They were joking, but Zac knew the thought of him not coming back was painful for Jenny.

The two of them walked outside to the waiting stage. Zac tossed his well-worn saddle and saddlebags on top of the old Concord. He always made it a point to carry the beat-down saddle. It was like a well-broke-in chair, and the wear of the leather made it much less likely to squeak at the wrong time. Besides, between stages, trains, and rented horses, the feel of the familiar was not something he wanted to shun.

"I have something for you, Zac." She turned to face him and took his hand. "It has a sentimental value to me. I gave it to my fiance just before his last voyage. I don't know how Captain Hogan came across it, but he returned it to me when I walked over to his table in there. I never thought I'd see it again and I want you to have it."

"Jen, you got no call to give me anythin'."

"Zac Cobb, I won't take no for an answer."

"I can't be takin' anything from you, Jenny. Little women things are too easy to lose."

"Just put it on your watch chain as a reminder

to come home." Jenny ignored his protest and reached into her apron. Palming her treasure, she slipped it into his duster pocket.

"Don't look at it now. I'd be too embarrassed to have you open it while I'm standing here." Stepping back, she murmured, "Godspeed, Zachary Cobb."

He nodded and swung himself through the doors of the coach. With a whistle from Shorty and the crack of his twelve-foot whip, the team lunged forward and Zac pressed his hand into the door frame to keep from catapulting into the laps of the family seated across from him.

He watched the men emerge from the cafe and saw Captain Hogan step forward to distract Jenny as the coach pulled away. The dust of the stage blotted out the remains of the street as the wheels crunched and spun their way onto the main road east.

Sliding his hand into the duster, he felt for Jenny's remembrance. Slowly, he slipped the chain out. It was a gold locket. Opening it up, he saw a portrait of Jenny. Her smile and penetrating look warmed him. He snapped it shut and stared at the outside lid.

What he saw troubled him. He'd seen it before. It was the same locket he had left on Jeff's desk the afternoon before, one of the items taken from the pockets of the sailors he had killed on the Cambria road.

CHAPTER 3

His last goodbyes to Jenny, and the general po-
liteness he always practiced, had condemned him
to the center seat. Dust filled the coach and he
couldn't even see the road ahead. Zac had grown
far too many rough spots on his rear, courtesy of
Concord coach seats. Shorty's ability in piloting
that wheeled cradle carried him into every hole
in the road, it seemed. It didn't help that Zac had
his tailbone on the interior center seat. He was
facing a rearward cloud of belching dust and feeling each sudden jolt.

He'd have been all too happy to spell the two
barbed-wire drummers out on the top, but they
were in the open air for a good reason. Too much
whiskey mixed with some over-ripe pork con-
sumed the night before demanded they sit up
there facing the rear wheels. Until they recovered,
Zac had to content himself with encountering
each boulder in the road before he could see it
coming.

Every bone-crunching jar tossed the customers
first into the air, then across the coach. Each
passenger on board soon became thoroughly familiar with the knees, elbows, breath, and various
smells of their traveling companions. Every ride
he took convinced Zac about the future demise

of the company's passenger service. The railroad would be a welcome relief for almost everyone. He was headed for Visalia and knew that with a new railhead there, his rump could look forward to more promising accommodations.

The assortment of passengers on the stage included a woman and her two small children who were beginning a trip back to Boston. They were sitting on the backseat facing forward, and the woman's knees were embarrassingly banging into Zac's on occasion. They had chosen to travel by stage instead of ship because, as she explained to Zac, she "frequently became seasick." Unfortunately, the stagecoach was a fair rendition of rounding the Horn in the jaws of a storm even on a level road. Zac watched her blanch with each jolt and sag of the leather undercarriage.

In spite of their mother's discomfort, the children were enjoying the trip immensely. Their laughter made Zac's mind drift back to his own childhood. He smiled as they stepped on his toes and climbed onto his lap for a better view of the road. Occasionally, he would hold on to them while they poked their heads out the window to enjoy the rushing wind. Their mother was embarrassed, but Zac only smiled and politely agreed to be the children's anchor.

"Don't you let those rascals of mine continue to bother you, Mr. Cobb."

"Oh, it's all right, ma'am. Playing with children is something that's a rarity for me and it brings back happy memories."

The woman covered her mouth with her handkerchief, trying to stifle her queasiness. "You must have a wife and some children of your own, then."

"No, ma'am," he said. "I haven't afforded myself the luxury of that yet."

"You must have had a happy childhood home then, Mr. Cobb."

"Well, I must admit, ma'am, in Georgia where I came from, being a child before the war was pure pleasure. It was hard work too. Mostly though, it was imagination and play."

The woman smiled, and Zac could see the conversation was helping to settle her stomach. He went on, "Every tree used to be a castle and the mule was a steed armored for combat." He paused and smiled. "The mind is a fanciful thing for children," he said. "It's a shame we lose that kind of innocence."

The woman continued to hold her hand up to her mouth and nodded in his direction. "A mother has to feed that childlike imagination with good reading. I'm sure you had a mother who read to you, Mr. Cobb."

"Yes, ma'am, she read the Bible to us at night. There were also ample doses of poetry for us younguns, along with the writings of Sir Walter Scott."

"It sounds like you had a wonderful family. Do you still write to them? You know, a mother and father need to hear from their children, no matter how old they get." Zac sat quietly, thinking back.

It was a long silence that appeared to fluster the woman. "Did I say something wrong?" she asked.

Apologetically, he answered, "I'm sorry, ma'am, my mind drifted there for a moment. No, my folks are dead." There was a long, reflective pause. "I'm afraid death was a frequent visitor to my home."

"I'm sorry to bring up such an unpleasant memory for you, Mr. Cobb. I meant no harm by it."

"Oh, it's not that unpleasant; death comes to everyone and every family. The only issue is when and how." Zac went on, not knowing why he felt the need to talk to a perfect stranger. Maybe he felt he could tell his feelings to a woman who was safe for him. He knew he'd be getting off the stage and this woman couldn't bring the subject up again. Perhaps he just needed someone to understand him.

"At our home," he said, "death always came in the door masquerading as a relative from a ways off. You know, one that didn't live with us, but belonged when he came to visit." He paused and thought. He knew Jenny would give anything to hear his thoughts on this or any other subject, but something kept him bottled up around her. Yet, now, to a woman whose children had reminded him of his past, he was telling everything.

"I had two brothers and three sisters who didn't see their eighth birthday at my home, childhood illnesses and such. That kindly old grandfather death would pay us one of his visits. He'd sit at the table, pat us on the knee, and then promise to come back soon."

"Why, Mr. Cobb, I perceive you to be a philosopher and a deeply spiritual man. Are you a minister of the gospel?"

Zac grinned. "No, ma'am, not hardly." He patted the Shopkeeper Colt he was carrying in a shoulder holster under his arm. "This is my Bible nowadays."

"You surprise me, sir," she said. "You seem like such a gentle man, I'd never take you as one prone to violence."

Zac looked her in the eye. "I don't reckon I'm suited to violence on the inside. Peace is very important to my soul. I suppose I've just been on a quest for justice for so long and I've been using" — he slapped his underarm holster — "this type of thing to get it since I was sixteen. Now, it's kinda become my nature."

"I don't believe that for a moment, Mr. Cobb. I think your nature is deeper than that. It's somewhere back in your roots, Mr. Cobb, the place where your mother planted the Scriptures in your heart."

There was a pause and Zac continued to silently stare at the woman. For the first time in a long time, he thought about the spaces in his life that his job and his own personal need to set wrong things right had created. He knew, though, that deep down he wanted a quality to life that he no longer believed was possible — for him.

"You should turn your heart and your mind

41

back to your roots, Mr. Cobb. You can begin again. You can be anything you want to be."

"No, I suppose I'm just an expert on the subject of death. When a body's stood by and watched quietly while little boxes are lowered into the ground, something changes inside of him, I guess." He looked out the open window, and then into the eyes of the mother. "I've stood singing, praying, and listening to the words of Scripture over a lot of boxes." Zac settled into icy silence, listening to the wheels of the coach. The boyhood of his memories was now under the lilies, and he hadn't told the woman the half of it.

There had been a civility and even a gentle kindness to the graves behind his boyhood home, but there was no kindness in death during the war. The scars the battle left in his soul were the part of his life he couldn't put to rest. The torment went on, silent and unspoken. Memories of it still gave him nightmares. Whatever business he was in at any moment only served to deaden the pain he felt on the inside.

Shallow holes had been filled with the corpses of boys he'd eaten with the night before. Death came like clouds of devilish bats swooping down on waves of young men who were each expecting it without embracing it. Even now, the thought of it made him feel hard and cold inside.

He had seen what the war had done also on the walk home from Appomattox, a bereavement of spirit without the benefit of bodies. The hastily printed parole papers and the bitterness of that road left memories that time never seemed to cure. His soul was filled with the images of hollow eyes, the eyes of the ones left behind, the hungry, crying children and the burning tears of widows working in spring fields alone. They had stared silently, watching him from a distance, trying to see if he had the familiar look in his trudge that they had each long been waiting to see. In the end, when he walked by, they just kept standing silently in their fields. Fields that would soon belong to victorious strangers.

"Surely, Mr. Cobb, you're not all alone." The woman abruptly interrupted his thoughts. "You must have had brothers and sisters or relatives you could call your own."

"No, ma'am, I'm afraid I haven't. I spent several months after the war starin' down an empty road waitin' for three brothers to come back. Julian, Joe, and James had a two-year start on me in that war.

"I never did hear from them after I went to join up." He sighed. "When I got back, I'd drift into town and look over casualty lists or stare at the post box for a while. In the end, I just couldn't wait any longer. I had to sell what was left before the carpetbaggers took the place for taxes. I didn't have any more time left — or any hope, for that matter."

The children climbed over his lap again and poked their heads out the window. They laughed and pointed at the cattle on the hill and the sight of calves with their mothers. Zac smiled and thought how strange it was to be talking about death to a perfect stranger while holding her two sturdy children. It wasn't seemly, he thought.

It was a subject he lived with inside his head; though seldom, if ever, did he let what was in his head go directly to his mouth. He knew that with his job he had to know how to dish out death by the double handful. As a youngster, death had been a houseguest. As a soldier he had been its minister, a co-worker of hot lead and cold steel. He'd been persuaded during the war that death was an instrument of the holy cause. To "defy your foe no matter what the odds" was a creed spawned in him as a child. There was never any regard to the cost of honorable defiance. Death was simply the end of a life well lived and a cause worth defending.

In his childhood, Jesus had supervised a death accompanied by songs, tender smiles, and affectionate touches, but the devil had been its commander during his manhood. It came during those years with sudden surprise, with fear, and with the cold, cold ground of northern Virginia.

He watched the woman remove a worn Bible from her travel bag and open it up to read.

"Mr. Cobb, this book assures me there's always hope." She paused and spoke quietly. "I'm sure your mother would have said the same thing."

Zac remained silent. He'd said more than enough already. As a boy, he'd listened to enough of the Bible to respect a God who providentially administered the affairs of men and nations. War,

44

battle, and justice were struggles that involved a price. He knew he could live with that. What he couldn't live with was the pain of little boxes. The type of family death that tried to comfort someone with songs, yet took the life and hope out of him, that was what he wanted to avoid. He knew that to escape that type of pain, he had to evade the attachments of a home: no more family, no more family funerals.

"You tell me, Mr. Cobb, if the children are disturbing you."

"No, they're fine, ma'am." Zac smiled as the gentle lady again tried to balance herself in the seat. "It's the absence of children hereabouts that disturbs me most. I do admire a family with the courage to travel."

He leaned his head out the window to catch a look at the road up ahead, then barked out a plea to Shorty, " 'Bout time to stretch the legs!"

The old man growled back, "Just up ahead, keep your britches on."

Zac looked out at the rolling hills that separated the coast from the farms and ranches of the valley. A thick carpet of golden grass covered the hills, and bees floated over layers of blue, purple, and yellow flowers. Black oaks spotted an otherwise treeless terrain.

Occasionally, he could see a plowed field or herd of cattle through the jolting window. Times were changing, and California was filling up with strangers. Trains were choking the land, and the hoards of human locusts were slowly chewing up the best of the land and spitting out barbwire as their droppings.

"Whoa there," yelled Shorty as he pulled the team of horses to the side of the road. The children piled out of the coach, squealing and laughing as they ran to inspect the road.

"You children be careful out there. Don't go too far." The woman's voice rose with a hint of anxiety, and Zac smiled at the sound and memory of motherhood.

He stepped out ahead of the farmers and merchants who filled the tight box, then stood beside the door and offered his hand to the lady. Having helped her to the ground, he unlimbered his muscles and swung his arms to stave off the effects of the long ride. Walking to the rear of the coach, he lit his pipe.

"Mr. Cobb, that pipe smells lovely. I can't say as I see those all too often, but when I do, it reminds me of home. My father smoked one."

"Why, thank you, ma'am. Things that smell good are all around you here in California. You and your children sure beautify the smells inside of that coach." He drew a puff from the bowl and looked down the road at the children at play. "That little girl of yours, ma'am — Amy, is it?"

"Yes, that's right."

"She reminds me very much of my sister Dora May at that age. Same curls. Same smile."

The woman shifted under her full skirt as she turned back and stretched. She dabbed her forehead with a lace handkerchief clutched to her palm. "I can understand you having to leave your home, Mr. Cobb. What I heard of the Reconstruction was awful; but tell me, what made you decide to come to California?"

Zac stopped to relight his pipe and turn his gaze from the children to the woman who appeared intent on exploring his past. "Ma'am, when I left, there wasn't a home to leave. It was only a house surrounded by graves."

He poked the match flame down the bowl of his briar. Friends knew he lit his pipe when he didn't want to talk; it gave him something to do with his mouth besides form words. Today, it didn't seem to be working.

"I don't know why I decided to keep movin' on to the Pacific Coast. Maybe it was the strangeness and newness of the place. I guess it was the fartherest point I could go from where I started. The Mexicans owned most of the land when I got here, but times were changin' and those good folks were played out."

The smoke rose from the mixture as Zac eyeballed the hills. "My daddy's old place in Georgia is owned now by the winners of my war. Guess it's only proper I should get fixed into the land belongin' to the losers of my daddy's war."

The buzz of loud rattles and the screams of the children brought every head around with a jerk. "Snake! Snake! Rattlesnake!" The little boy ran back to the coach in a panic. All eyes turned to the little girl, who had fallen away from the snake and into the rocks behind her.

She froze in terror while the creature coiled to strike. Zac ran to the rocks where the children had been playing, then replaced his six-gun in his holster. The chance of a ricochet made the shot far too risky.

He slid the blade of his Bowie knife out from its sheath and raised a hand to get Amy's attention. "Sweetheart, just lie still. Don't try to move."

The serpent coiled, ready to strike. Amy pressed her back into the sharp rocks and gasped for breath. Zac could see the panic in the girl's eyes and was afraid any sudden movement from her would produce a strike. Knowing rattlers strike at movement, he had to try to keep her very still and calm.

"Amy, just pretend you're part of the rock. Don't move, darlin'. I won't let it hurt you."

She raised her eyes from the snake and forced a smile. Zac ran swiftly toward her and clamped his boot on to the rattler. He pressed the shining blade into the snake's neck and snapped off its hissing head with one stroke. He scooped Amy into his arms, stepped over the twitching body of the dead snake, and laid the frightened girl into her mother's arms. "She's scared, but she'll be all right," he said.

He motioned for the boy to come over and watch while he stripped the skin off of the still warm snake. "Here, this skin can be a keepsake for you, boy. Don't be afraid. This thing's still movin', but he's very dead." He picked up the

48

pany is mixed up with this, someone who knew what they wanted and when and where to get it. No passengers were robbed, no coaches without payrolls stopped, no mail pouches taken. Meetin' an armed coach with only four or five holdup men shows they weren't expectin' a great force of arms. No, these boys knew what they were doin'. They knew 'cause they had good information."

Zac gazed at the map with "X's" on its surface that lay under the pile of papers. "I'm guessin' these fellas are holed up in the mountains around the pass. Word on the shipments can't go much faster than the coach itself."

Wooster scratched his head. "I'm sure we can round up a posse in Calico. Those folks have been smarting from a lack of cash, and they'd go after those boys with a good collection of hemp."

Cobb cocked his head and stared at the full-bellied Wooster. He was a little irritated that the agent hadn't followed his reasoning. He spoke firmly. "The head, Jerry, the head! No, I've got to go all the way to San Bernardino, then ride the line. I've got to make sure everybody who shouldn't know I'm on that stage does know. I've got to see this man eyeball to eyeball. The one who is the head has to strike first; then I can cut it off."

CHAPTER 4

Jenny opened the back door of the cafe, stamping the dirt from her heels. "Me Che." The call in the dark went unanswered, and Jenny noticed the cold stove as she removed her jacket. The oversight would have gone unnoticed with most anyone else, but Me Che was always there with the stove hot and the eggs gathered before Jenny or George, the cook, arrived. It was unlike her to be late.

With hands trembling from the chill of the morning, she found the matches and scratched the side of the old stove, using the flame to poke the kindling that had been carefully laid out the night before. She took the remainder of the match and found the wick of the lamp, then quickly carried it to the pump to draw water for coffee. Walking back to the stove, she spotted Me Che cowering at the door. The girl remained outside in the disappearing darkness, wringing both hands and looking up at Jenny through her dark bangs.

"I solly, Miss Jenny. I late. Peese, may I go work?"

Jenny grinned and clapped her hands together several times. "Of course, girl. Get in here and let's go. Everybody is late sometime, you too, I suppose." The girl scurried to the cupboard and quietly and quickly removed several baskets.

"It not hoppon again, Miss Jenny. I go get cheeken eggs." With that the back door screeched and slammed, and Jenny heard the rocky dirt crunching loudly beneath the departing steps of the shamefaced girl.

Increasingly, the regulars of the cafe were being joined by railroad officials and those who were doing business with the railroad, and that business was booming. The morning passed quickly in the cafe with a busyness that brought sweat in the kitchen and on Jenny and Me Che as they ran in and out through the kitchen doors to serve their customers.

Jenny noticed a distracted look on Me Che, who looked past those who were seated to watch new people who were arriving. Several spills, and the hurriedness of her young helper, alerted Jenny to the fact that all was not right. The volume of business, however, made discussion impossible. Besides, even on slow days, Jenny couldn't seem to make conversation with Me Che.

Captain Hogan came in around nine and took his usual seat with the railroad men he was arranging to supply. Jenny listened to his order and rushed to the kitchen to pass on the late arriver's request. "I take hot coffee to hem, Missy." And with that, Me Che burst through the door and carried a hot pot along with eating utensils.

In a matter of moments there was a crash in the dining room accompanied by screams and loud yelling. Jenny and George rushed from the kitchen to see the men at the corner table wrestling on the floor with the distraught waitress. Amid shouts from the men about the girl, the young Chinese woman was screaming, "Where is my brother? You murderer. What have you done to him? You killed my brother."

Slumped glassy-eyed into his chair was Mike Hogan, a butcher knife handle protruding from his upper right shoulder. "I'm all right," he croaked. "Get the doctor and pull this thing out, but do it . . . very . . . slowly."

Me Che lay on her cell bunk staring at the ceiling when Jenny came through the door of Jeff Bridger's office. Never had Jenny seen her so motionless and absorbed. She acted like a corpse that breathed.

All hopes and dreams for her new world and new life were crushed. Whatever future she had imagined for herself in America was spilled with the coffee and Mike Hogan's blood on the floor of the diner.

Jeff stood up and stepped away from the papers on his desk. His six-foot-five-inch frame and broad shoulders showed that he was more accustomed to the heavy work around his ranch than he was to sitting behind a desk. Rawhide gloves dangled from his waist and dust covered his scuffed boots.

He'd worn out the seat of his trousers, so his wife had repaired them with a large buckskin patch. All morning he had caught himself fidgeting in his chair. The patch made him feel slightly uncomfortable. It reminded him of the feeling of being in the saddle even while he was sitting behind the desk. He had taken the sheriff's job for the same reason Zachary Cobb was working for Wells Fargo: The steady cash made growing a ranch more promising. It also made providing for a wife and five children, even in bad times, a little more doable.

"I can't get a thing outa her, Jenny," he said. "She was screaming at the top of her lungs about her brother being murdered when they drug her down the street, but since I closed the door on her, she's been just like you see. Can you see if you can prod her into talking? I can't help her if I don't know where to look."

Bridger opened the cell door and Jenny carried a stool into the damp iron cage. Sitting beside her disheartened waitress, she fumbled for words. "Me Che, I know you don't know me very well. Perhaps you don't even trust me." The young girl's eyes blinked and tears began to form. "But, I trust you," Jenny said. "You've worked out just wonderfully at the cafe. I've trusted you enough to give you a key to the place, and I've never been disappointed in you."

Tears began to run over the prone girl's cheeks. Jenny made no motion except to reach out her hand and gently place it on the edge of the bed. She became more deliberate with each word she formed. "Right now, Me Che, I am your only friend in this town. I promise I will help you all I can, but you've got to trust me and tell me the truth."

The tearful girl turned her head away from Jenny to face the wall. Minutes passed silently, while Jenny waited for a response. She couldn't see the girl's glistening eyes, but shortly heard quiet sobs. "I so ashamed," the girl croaked out. "I bring dishonor upon you, Miss Jenny. I can hurt you no more here."

Jenny reached out and wrapped her fingers around Me Che's hand. "You won't hurt me. I just want to help you."

Me Che turned to face Jenny, fresh tears puddling up in her eyes. "That sailor man is a bad man. He your friend. How can you believe me if I tell you?"

"Me Che, perhaps you are mistaking him for someone else. You are strange to our country. Maybe you don't know what you are saying."

The frail girl's almond eyes hardened behind her tears. "I know that man. I no make mistake. He bring me here on his ship last year. He shame me. He hurt me. He give my brother the opium, and now, he kill him. I no make mistake."

Jenny's hand swiftly pulled back to cover her mouth, and her eyes widened as Me Che turned back to face the wall. Jenny swallowed hard, her mind tumbling over the things she knew about Mike Hogan and what she knew about the dependable nature of her young Chinese waitress. If Jenny couldn't believe her story, no one could.

If she could believe it, she might be the only one in town who would.

There was a large contingent of the townspeople who were highly resentful of the industrious Chinese, and Jenny had no desire to be saddled with the responsibility of opposing alone a town full of hatred for these immigrant workers. People were irritated because the Chinese stayed mostly to themselves, and the townspeople especially resented the immigrants' thrift. There were rumors that some ate mice rather than shop for food.

Even the appearance and manners of the foreigners went against the townspeople. The inherent courtesy and dignity of the Chinese were often interpreted as signs of deviousness and sinister character.

Being alone after the news that her fiance's ship had been lost had chilled Jenny's soul to the bone. It was the exact feeling she'd left San Francisco to escape, and now what she might be forced to do in supporting this young woman could easily drive a wedge between her and the community she had learned to love.

But Jenny was courageous. She took in stray cats that others kicked aside, and that fact of her character wasn't going to change. She had taken a risk in hiring Me Che. Many of the townspeople objected to having a Chinese girl handle their food. There had always been first, second, and third looks when the girl served them. Jenny found it hard to believe what Me Che had said about her fiance's old friend Mike Hogan, but it was plain to see the girl believed it.

It took very little convincing for Jenny to persuade Jeff Bridger to follow up on the young woman's accusations. She was equally persuasive as to how much she trusted Mike Hogan. "Jeff, this man is a ship's master. He is used to accepting his duty and not blinking an eye. I just know if he was the type of friend that my Henry would have as a mate on his ship, he can be trusted. There must be some logical explanation."

Bridger reached to the wooden peg for his gun and holster and strapped it to his waist. "Jenny girl, I'll do a little digging. That's my job. But the Chinese don't trust anyone with round eyes, and I guess we've given them plenty of reason not to. This star on my chest is going to make me even more unpopular, but I'll do my best."

The Chinese section of town was abuzz with the news of the morning, and Jeff could sense the fear in people's eyes as he attempted to ask questions. He knew his size intimidated all but a few of the Anglos who lived nearby and he towered above the Chinese. He looked down at them with strange blue eyes and felt that in this part of town the star he carried on his chest seemed to shine like the sun.

He spoke a little Arapaho, did very well with Paiute, but the strange language that bent around his ears in Hop alley seemed to him like a catastrophe of moans accompanied by the breaking of dinnerware. Jeff had been nowhere else in his life that he felt more peculiar or out of place. Only three blocks from his office, this part of town seemed like the backside of the moon.

His questions about Me Che's brother were met with blank, silent gawks; and when he walked away, the following palaver was voiced with a fever pitch that was animated and intense. While he couldn't understand the words that were being spoken, he could understand the tone. It was gossip mixed with worry and accompanied by hatred. Mentally, he filled in the meaning. The thought of carrying on an investigation in this part of town was beyond him, but he had promised Jenny and that was enough.

Group after huddling group, he asked the same questions and got the same fearful responses. However, it was after he had waylaid his third or fourth bunch of passersby that he noticed her. She was an old woman. The age of Orientals was hard for Jeff to figure, but her gray hair pulled back in a bun and her stooped, plodding gait put her in her late sixties at least, he figured.

In each successive group he talked to, he spotted her at the edge of the crowd, just standing, listening quietly. Several times they made eye contact, only to have her drop her chin and stare at the dirt. As he continued his futile march down the street, he occasionally paused and fabricated a look of interest in one of the shop windows, all the while trying to spot the old woman from the corner of his eye.

She clogged along in an elongated black dress,

keeping a distance behind him, and would attempt to hide in the shadows when he stopped,
pretending to take in the sights of the street. The
other people Jeff talked to wasted little time in
departing from him, and had even less desire to
be seen with him, but this old lady kept up a
distant but interested chase.

He deliberately sought out a corner and, rounding it, glanced around to assure himself that no
one was watching. Then, when he could safely
persuade himself that he was out of the old
woman's sight, he turned to wait for his elderly
pursuer.

She rounded the corner, head down, and
screeched to a halt with arms flailing from the
sudden, frightful sight of the big lawman staring
down at her.

"Pardon me, ma'am. Can I help you?" She
seemed to topple backward at suddenly being
confronted. Bridger reached out to steady her.
Gulping, she dashed quick glances from side to
side and then at the ground.

"You want know Me Low?"

"Yes, ma'am," Bridger replied, "if he is Me
Che's brother. I am trying to help her."

The old lady cocked her gray head backward
and looked at him. "I know. I hear you good man.
They my grandchilds. Wait, slow come to me. I
show."

Jeff could only guess that the old lady meant
for him to follow her, and by her actions it was
obvious she didn't want him to follow too closely.

He watched her amble around the corner before he slowly and discreetly began to pace off the backsides of the busy Chinese shantytown.

The tension on the street at the sight of his passing made him feel a stranger in the town he was sworn to protect. He had been in many villages of the Arapaho as a young man and felt the glow of a simple people there. But here, he sensed no welcome, no warmth. Perhaps the ancient culture of the Chinese made them more complicated. He knew their history went far beyond his own. Jeff was educated enough to know that when his ancestors had been clubbing people with stones and eating raw meat, these people had developed literature, music, and poetry, and served delicacies in fragile ceramics. He respected them, but he knew he'd have to earn their respect.

The old woman's age showed as she walked tediously straight ahead, eyes firmly fixed to the dirt in front of her, neither speaking to anyone nor being spoken to. All at once she stopped and stood gazing at a two-story yellow house with a lacquered and shiny red door. It was squashed between the tenements of the back street. She seemed to sigh, then turned to make eye contact with Jeff. Suddenly, as if thirty years of age had flown away from her, the old woman scampered down the alleyway to her left and vanished.

Jeff dashed down the street to be sure he wouldn't lose her, but, arriving at the alley, he saw only washpots, crying children, and pigtailed men stirring laundry. There was no sign of the old woman. Retracing his path, he paused at the steps to the yellow building with the shiny red door. Something told him that was where he should start.

CHAPTER 5

Bridger pushed his way into the Wo Fat Market. It was the building that butted up next to the yellow two-story the old woman had seemed to direct him to. Somehow, he could not bring himself to walk up the stairs and simply knock on the front door of the house. He wanted to find another entrance, one that would allow him to enter unnoticed. The proximity of the houses allowed no alley on that side of the street, and he was hoping to move through the market and find an exit to the alley out back.

Customers who were leaving stood by in disbelief as the big man smiled and pushed past the hanging strands of black and red beads, which served to keep out the flies and still allow a breeze. Dust clouds of flour and strange smells of Jasmine filled the small store, and a bit of light filtered in around the ducks that hung in the window. Shoppers stopped cold in their tracks, their hands to their sides as Jeff smiled in an attempt to mollify their fears. It was difficult to blend in and there was nowhere to hide; there was also no back door.

He had noticed, though, a side door, which obviously led to the house that was his objective. "Excuse me," Bridger said. "I need to go next door. Does this door work?" He'd never been known for his subtlety, and quietly seeking entrance to a house through a side door in a busy Chinese market was a method of investigation he knew would never be taught to Pinkerton agents.

He shook the brass knob and got no movement from the locked door. Holding up a plaintive palm, he feigned polite helplessness at the situation, one which genuinely reflected a feeling he'd had in their section of town all morning.

Only gazes of fear and misunderstanding came from the clerks, who, like the customers, stood with their hands pinned to their sides and continued to watch with mouths open.

Bridger again tried turning the knob. "Is there a key to this door?" he asked. Only stunned, silent stares met his question.

The sheriff shrugged and, with a boyish grin, forced his shoulder against the locked door. The jamb splintered from the blow and the wall shook under the power of his two-hundred-pound-plus muscular body. He turned to apologize, only to be greeted with loud chatter and an aproned shopkeeper waving a key that was no longer needed. "Sorry. I'll replace it. I'll get it fixed."

What a fine way to enter the house unnoticed, he thought.

Pivoting, he scanned a railing and stairs that led to what was obviously the next-door basement. Bridger took a match from his pocket, raked it along the red brick wall, and closed what was left of the door. The shouts, chatter, and whispers died down as he stepped away from the pandemonium and edged his way down the rickety stairs, one soft step at a time.

The cool dirt basement floor had a path to and from the market that was worn and well packed. A lamp hung from one of the supporting posts and Bridger removed the mantle and lit it. The match had burned down to his fingers before the wick glowed with a rising flame. He dropped the smoldering match to the floor, putting his fingers to his mouth to extinguish the pain.

Holding the glowing lamp high, he could see boxes and bails that lined the walls of the basement. Large crates that were suitable for shipping seemed to litter the ground.

The light filtered through the cracks of the floor above him, accompanied by a noise he had never heard before. It was like the sound of humming male voices. No one tune could be distinguished. In fact, as Bridger listened carefully he didn't think any tune was being mimicked whatsoever. The voices meshed into a low moan of contentment, a groan of satisfaction that was otherworldly, Gothic.

Bridger slid his hand along the rail that led to the floor above. The sound continued to drift through the walls but seemed to come from behind him as he pushed open the basement door of the yellow house.

Strange mats and rugs lay on the floors with dangling lamps that cast a cherry hue of soft, glowing light. Bridger noticed that the window of the front door, down the hall to the left, had been painted a scarlet color. Then he realized that all the windows had been painted a deep red, so that even in bright daylight there was perpetual darkness in the house. Of course, even the paint could not keep the glow of light from penetrating the uneven brush strokes on the glass.

A sickening but sweet smell seemed to come from the direction of the muted hum. Gliding down the hall to his right, Bridger placed his hand on the door that seemed to contain the fearsome secret he had been smelling and hearing since entering the house. The frames of the thin door were warm to the touch and he twisted the knob, gently pushing it open.

Belching forth from the room came a cloud of smoke like nothing Bridger had ever seen or smelled. *Opium,* he thought. *A celestial house of leisure. The opium downstairs and the women above.* Bridger had only heard about this place from a few of the men in town who had tried the upstairs delights. In the Chinese community, the younger men seemed to prefer the stairs, while the older, wealthier men stayed content below. He pushed past the first stench and tried to accustom his eyesight and his breathing.

The room was large, with small dangling lanterns hanging from a grass matted ceiling. Unoccupied pads littered the floorspace and platforms displayed men smoking long pipes. Every man's eyes seemed shrunk into his skull, and after puffing on the pipe, each man held his wind, releasing smoke while humming a breathy moan. The frail forms seemed lifeless, their hands limply caressing the pipe, their slippered feet curled up behind them in a ball. Not one eye moved in Bridger's direction; each man continued in the careful contemplation of his own mystical inner world.

The wall nearest Jeff was arrayed with pegs that held hats and silk jackets, while a hollow petrified foot of what he could only guess had been an elephant was studded with walking sticks of every description. He carefully edged forward toward the center of the room. His jaw hung limp, gazing in wonder and drinking in the passive evil that seemed frozen into the texture of the room. This was a place of awakened sleep, an avenue to deaden the pain of hard labor in a strange new world.

Stooping and reaching down to one of the candy-apple painted platforms, Bridger picked up a smooth leather bag. The opium powder clung crystallized to the inner seams.

As he dropped the bag he lifted his fingers to his nose. *Whale oil?* He couldn't remember a whaler putting in to the coast in some time, but he'd trimmed enough wicks with it to know what he was wiping on his lapels.

Looking around the room, he shook his head. The cry of "gold" had drained the labor pool for the railroads, and these people had been brought in from the Far East to fill the void. They arrived in waves by ship in such numbers that the immigration of the Chinese had been stopped. The smuggling in of these people continued, however, to small ports like Cambria and Moro Bay, which were less noticeable and perhaps more desirable, becoming the routes of choice. Labor riots had broken out in many cities during the bad economic times people were currently experiencing, and full-scale racial wars seemed to be a regular occurrence in California.

Every theft on the coast was blamed on the Chinese, and in some towns the lawmen themselves had led vengeful citizens in tearing down the Orientals' houses and supervising lynchings. At the very least, local political leaders stirred the pots and ripped open pillows for tar-and-feather orgies. To Bridger, it seemed ironic that so many had died in this country to free black slaves, only to see the victors import other slaves to do their work.

The skulls of passivity all around the sheriff patiently sucked at their pipes while the big man moved past them. His hair stood on end as the sweet smell filled his mustache. Lifting his head, he saw two young Chinese men, stripped to the waist, enter from a door across the room. One carried a stout fighting pole. They began to step over drowsy old men as they separated and spread out around the sheriff.

Stepping backward, Bridger was alarmed by the sound of the door behind him closing. Quickly, he swung his head to see two other fighters, one armed with a sharp-pointed broadsword.

The swordsman latched the door, then turned on his heels to point his weapon at the lawman.

Deliberately, Bridger had drawn his Peacemaker, but pointing it toward the swordsman as a show of force brought a quick response.

The pole that had been carried into the room came crashing down from behind on Bridger's wrist, sending the revolver spinning along the hardwood floor. He had not noticed the circle around him tightening, nor seen the menace on his right hand, until it was too late.

"I'm not looking for trouble. I am looking for information," Bridger said, trying to sound composed.

The one with the sharp-edge sneered. "You found all the information you gonna get, round-eye." He spat out the final, halting phrase, "All the trouble, too!"

With a jerk of elbows and knees, the shirtless disciple next to the swordsman flew through the air and landed a flying kick into Bridger's solar plexus. The big man had braced himself for the blow and, scrambling to his feet, found himself the target of new blows from the young man's feet and fists. Had Bridger been the size of his opponents, each punch would have had calamitous impact.

He had the bulk, but neither that factor nor the star he wore in his chest discouraged his attackers in the least. For a big man, though, he was surprisingly nimble.

The time he had put into prizefighting in the gold camps before settling down on the coast had not been in vain. He had lost little of his skill, and ducking under another swing, he landed a hard punch into the young man's middle that drove the air from his opponent's lungs with a "whoosh."

As another fighter approached him, the sheriff noticed from his peripheral vision the warrior with the stick begin to rush him from behind. Waiting until the last split second he ducked, vaulting his assailant off his back and into the approaching fighter. A swift but solid kick to the head put the attacker out of business.

Bridger picked up the discarded staff and spun swiftly to face the approaching swordsman. To his left, he came down hard on the neck of the man struggling to crawl out from beneath his companion. He then immediately swung the rod, bashing the head of the breathless attacker on his right. All the while, his attention was riveted to the shining sword that spun toward him.

Circling to the left, Bridger tried to parry the first blow with his new weapon, only to see it sliced cleanly in two by the long blade. He smiled nervously. "I can see you're a man who takes care of his tools."

His remark only brought another swing, which Bridger escaped by stumbling back into the coat rack. Grabbing a jacket, he carefully wrapped his left arm in the wound silk. He would hate to have to fend off a blow with only that coat and the bone of his left arm, but if it came to that, he would.

The sword came slicing down and Bridger held

up the half of the pole he still carried. The blade cut through it like it was butter. Bridger's look of surprise at the smoothly sliced end as he dropped it brought a smile to his adversary's face.

The young man suddenly lunged at Bridger, who rolled his body across the coat-banked wall, tossing garments at the swordsman. The Chinese henchman struggled to extricate the point of his blade from the wooden wall, but the seconds it took to remove it produced a shower of black silk jackets.

Reaching into the elephant's foot, the sheriff retrieved a gnarled cane and smashed it into the young man's elbow as the assailant turned to shake off the clothing.

The blade hit the floor and Bridger sent a left hook into the man's face. The impact sounded like breaking glass. He picked the young man up and walked him across the room, dangling his slippered feet above the floor. Keeping his adversary suspended by a strong left arm, Bridger launched a cracking blow with the cane, finishing the job. "Nothing like the root of a crabapple tree," he said simply.

Dropping the stick, he raised his challenger by both hands, coming face-to-face with the young man. "Where is Me Low?" he demanded.

The opponent's eyes blinked at the sheriff's display of power. "He is dead," the man said.

"You know this for a fact? How did this happen?"

"He brought us the opium from the ships, so

we left his sister to work with you roundeyes. Then he not bring it. He work for railroad. They kill him and they defy the Tong. No one can defy the Tong and the Grandmaster. It is to die."

The young man's eyes burned into the sheriff's brain. "You, big man, you defy us, you will die too. No one can tear down what we build."

Bridger grunted, "We'll see. Let's start tearing down what you built by letting in some air." With that, he marched his accuser toward the painted window that glowed at the end of the room.

With his strong arms, Bridger vaulted the young man through the glass and watched him tumble down the outside stairs to the porch below. The spray of red glass littered the air and the landing of the house.

Turning to leave, Jeff watched the old men with their pipes pause and blink at the sunlight. Each cot continued to hum with a contentment that refused to acknowledge the war that had gone on in the room. Stooping down to retrieve his revolver, he heard the groan of one of his victims. Bridger yanked a pipe from one of the stupefied men and pushed it into the young man's mouth. "Here, you need this more than he does."

CHAPTER 6

Zac stepped down from the train in San Bernardino. Flat tile roofs and adobe walls baked in a sun that shimmered. Flowering vines climbed and tethered themselves to gleaming white fences. The mountains in the distance began to appear behind the ribbons of white clouds that streaked the sky. The desert winds had begun to blow and dry air stirred the dust in the streets.

To the north, Cajon Pass sliced through the mountains and meandered toward the mining areas of the Mojave. Several banks did their business with Wells Fargo, and the company carried the payrolls that allowed the men to go underground and the stamp mills to melt the silver of the desert into ingots for shipment.

Zac conferred with the agent in charge, Bill Sampson, a newcomer he knew little about, then he reserved a seat on the next northbound stage. He wore his dark suit and tie, taking care to strap on his under-the-shoulder holster and pin the "Special Agent" badge to his vest. Knowing he was on his way to the banks that Wells Fargo did business with in town, he carefully combed his hair. If he was going to sniff out the source of the information flowing to the bandits, he knew he had to look the part. It meant exposing and even quietly flaunting his identity. He knew it also involved assuring each bank officer that he himself would ride with the next shipment.

At the Mercantile Bank, a quiet clerk escorted him into the president's office. It was comfortably furnished with overstuffed cowhide sofas and an imposing bearskin rug. Behind the massive desk and to the rear of the bank president's chair stood a large grizzly bear, its massive arms raised menacingly and a permanent snarl emblazoned on its black lips.

Zac extended his hand to a man with an imposing black mustache who rose to greet him. "Good morning, Mr. Cobb. I am Jonas Patterson. I understand you will be protecting the bank's money tomorrow."

"You are well-informed, Mr. Patterson. I will go out with the coach in the mornin' and take it all the way to Calico."

Motioning to a seat in front of the desk, the lanky executive took a black cigar out of a porcelain bowl and offered one to Zac.

"Thank you, no," Zac said. "I've got my own habit makin's." The agent pulled out his pipe as they both sat down. "I see you're a hunter, Mr. Patterson."

The banker grinned and puffed on the fire at the end of the cigar. "Not actually, Mr. Cobb. I pay other people to do my hunting for me. I'm more a trophy collector." He blew a large cloud of black smoke and pointed toward the window with the lit cigar. "Our hills out there have more than gold in them. They have more than a few of these beasts still roaming around."

"Huntin' is a specialty of mine, Mr. Patterson," Zac said. "Only thing is, they hang my trophies from the gallows, or leastwise lock 'em away for a mighty long time."

The bank president cleared his throat. "I trust you'll not be disappointed on this trip, Mr. Cobb. We'll expect a good report."

He pushed a paper detailing the strongbox count across the desk toward the agent. "This shipment will make up for the last one lost to those holdup men. The miners up there missed their last payday and this one is already overdue. Forty thousand dollars is a lot of money. We'd send some outriders with the coach, but that would be tipping our hand."

Zac took out a match and popped a flame from the end of his thumbnail to light his pipe. "From what I hear, Mr. Patterson," — Zac puffed as the smoke rose — "the thieves seem to know the times of shipment with or without extra guards." The men each blew smoke at each other from across the desk.

"I understand you're from San Luis, Mr. Cobb. Beautiful country up there, and with the railroad coming in, it ought to boom. You're a mighty lucky man."

Zac carefully thought through what he had communicated since arriving in San Bernardino, and he knew his whereabouts and his home were not among the pertinent facts he'd let out.

"You seem to know much about the business of California, Mr. Patterson."

The mustached smoker drew closer to Zac to press home a point he was about to make. "The future of California is my business, Cobb. I pay close attention to the comings and goings of the rails. I believe this particular community will rise and fall on the strength of an eastbound railroad coming through San Bernardino."

Zac smiled. He pulled out his watch, with the locket Jenny had given to him freshly attached to the chain. Opening the watch, he raised his eyebrows, signaling that their time was up. The banker's eyes seemed drawn to the locket swinging on the gold chain. Replacing the watch in his pocket, Zac smiled. "Yes, Mr. Patterson, a railroad, and the enforcement of the laws against stage robbery."

"Oh, that too, Mr. Cobb, to be sure, that too."

The following morning, before daylight, Zac was in the livery stable buying horses. He knew at least one possible suspect had to be eliminated or confirmed and had thought things through on just how to do that. What he had in mind would mean shadowing the payroll; however, not riding in the coach with it.

Every banking official he had spoken to believed Cobb would be on that coach, but it was important that his best suspect knew that he wouldn't be. The man who had to be confirmed or eliminated as that nominee, for the sake of the company, was the agent in charge, Bill Sampson. He was the one man Zac could think of who had all of the information necessary to mastermind the robberies. Someone else might be responsible, but Sampson had to be purged as a candidate first.

Choosing an Appaloosa stud that looked well built for rough terrain, Zac saddled him with his old saddle and changed into his shotgun chaps, buckskin jacket, and rough boots. He also selected a large mare to spell the Appaloosa on the trail. Keeping up with a coach that had frequent changes in its team might require some doing and Zac liked to be prepared. He tied his side holster down, checked his loads and ammunition, and walked to the street-side office of Wells Fargo.

Zac stepped into Sampson's waiting room and the older man met him at the door. "Well, well, Cobb. You look fit for bronc bustin'." Zac slapped the dust from his leggings and swept his hat low, motioning to the inside office. Closing the door, Zac rested his rear on the desk and lifted each boot to the arm of the settee to strap on his spurs.

Zac began, "What I am goin' to tell you can't leave your own head." Sampson leaned forward on his elbows with interest. Zac pretended a nonchalant disinterest in the man's reaction as he continued to adjust his spurs, but kept the corner of his eye on the stationmaster's reaction. "I won't be on that stage today, but I will be close-by."

Sampson's jaw hung open. "I don't follow you,

Cobb. How you gonna catch those men if you're not on that stage?"

Zac buckled on his last spur. "Oh, I don't plan on catchin' 'em." He looked up into the station-master's face. "See, I plan on killin' 'em." Crossing his arms over his chest, Zac took a long look at the man and let his words sink in. "I'm plannin' on bein' close-by and carryin' enough fire power to take them down hard. Got my own forebodin' about who's in on these robberies, and everyone in town knows I'm gonna be on that stage. I think I'd sooner be watchin' it than be in it when those boys hit."

The hesitation in the stationmaster's voice was obvious. "Well, if that's your plan . . . we'd better round up a posse to go with you."

Zac wiped the inside of his hatband with a fresh handkerchief. "I work alone. That's the way I do what I do. More people involved just means more trouble as far as I'm concerned."

"Takes a great deal of sand to do that, Cobb."

Zac grinned and picked up a long-fringed buck-skin bag he had propped on the edge of the desk. "It won't take much sand," Zac said. "Just a good eye."

He slid the stock out of the rifle bag, showing the checkered grip and blue hammer of a Creed-more Sharps rifle. "I'll drop the first one before they hear the shot and get the second and third before they know where it's comin' from. After that, I'll just ride 'em down and get the rest one by one."

Swearing Sampson to silence, he rode out toward the pass and Mormon Rocks station, taking comfort from the mixed signals he'd sent out. If the stage passed through unmolested, there would be a stationmaster's job open in San Bernardino.

The hills stretched into flattened towers of rock and the holes in the Mormon Rocks whistled with wind that cut across them. Marmots hid in the shadows and scurried into cracks as Zac rode up to the station. Hitching the horses, he entered the dark dugout that served as stage station in the pass.

A savory venison stew was just coming to a boil in the iron pot that hung over the fire, and Zac settled down and was served in the corner across from a spent deck of cards. They seemed poorly hand-marked and well-serviced, but now lay in a blue pile. Three sweat-soaked miners stretched themselves across the bar, their backsides facing his direction.

The stationhand poured drinks for them, laughing and talking. Caked dirt on their clothes and what was to be seen of their hides gave them the appearance of erect and bearded alligators. As the middle one turned on his elbows, a broad smile crossed his face and the young man's bright gold tooth winked in Zac's direction.

"Looky here, Pa," he said. "We got us a card player." The others turned and stared at Zac, talking among themselves in low voices and laughing. Nodding to one another, they stomped toward the table. With his hat hung low over his eyes, Zac continued to spoon in the hot stew. The older man reached out to the blue deck with a chapped and gnarled hand.

"We'ze the McKenneys. Let's gamble a spell."

Zac removed his spoon and cocked his head up, studying the dirty intruders. "I'm finishin' my stew, then I'll be gone. Have to pass on y'all's game, boys."

The older brother with the big smile broke into a grin. "You're setten at our table, mister. This here is a card table, and before you get up and walk away from it, you're durn sure gonna have to play some cards."

The old man allowed a subtle sneer to cross his face. The bear claw necklace that hung loosely around his neck rattled as he swung his head around to look both his sons in the eye. "Now, boys, let's us be polite. If'n you want somethin', you has to go about it in the right way."

Turning to Zac, he spoke in a smooth voice, "We spend a lot of time in the hills, mister, and we seldom get to find someone fresh to play cards with. Now we've got plenty of gold we done dug out of our part of the earth, and you look like money to us and a fair afternoon's sport." Wrapping his mitt around a large Walker Colt and dragging it from his pants, the old man laid it on the table. "My boy here's right, though. Before you walk away, you're sure gonna have to play some cards."

Zac held the spoon to his mouth and gently blew on the stew. "I do rightly appreciate yer offer boys, but I'm busy today. You need to also understand something else." Zac's left hand was beneath the brown table, cradling the bag that carried his Creedmore. With his thumb, he cocked the heavy hammer. The sound of it carried a ring of authority as Zac continued to blow on the savory steam curling through his mustache.

"This Sharps can do a terrible thing to a man's kneecaps, and I've got it pointed at yours right now." Zac locked eyes with the old man. "If you don't turn around and walk back to that bar, you won't be walkin' anywhere again. You'll be scootin' up to this table on your rear end." The smiles quickly disappeared and the men's mouths hung open. "Now stick that horse pistol back in your pants and keep the hammer under that waistband." The dusty intruders turned silently away and walked back to the bar.

Moments later the sound of the stage overshadowed the men's murmurs. Fresh voices and new light poured into the dugout, and the long tables on the wall filled fast with passengers needing the hot stew. Two miners and a farmer with his boy, who looked to be about nine or ten, tore into the bread while the ladle from the iron pot dished out the leavings from the last deer kill.

Zac sipped some buttermilk as he watched the farmer pray silently with the little boy before they began to eat. The other passengers had busily begun making short work out of the stew.

During the meal, the boy scrambled free of his seat and went to eye a licorice jar. He fumbled in his pocket for traveling money, and a gleaming silver dollar fell to the floor and rolled along the length of the room before landing next to the foot of the youngest McKenney. The bearded drinker continued to slurp his whiskey, subtly shifting his foot to cover the child's treasure. "Excuse me, sss-sir," the boy spoke up. "I bbbb-believe my dollar is under your foot." Ignoring the boy, the stocky man stared into his glass and swigged it down.

The tall, blond farmer had quickly joined the boy and, pulling the lad aside, got down on one knee to face him. While the McKenneys wheeled and leaned back on their elbows to take in the room, the father spoke deliberately to his son, but with a tone loud enough for everyone to hear.

"Son, money is never worth the shame of fighting for that alone. Almost anything is more valuable than money. All the money in the world couldn't bring back your mother's life and none of it could buy your soul. We'll leave the dollar and keep our good sense."

With the young man in hand and without casting an eye in any direction, the farmer stood and steered his young pupil to what was left of their stew. Zac watched as the men at the bar turned their thoughts quickly back to the bottoms of their glasses.

As the passengers filed out to fill up the coach,

Zac glanced up to see one final educated look the young boy spent in the direction of the McKenneys. Rising and shouldering his saddlebags, he passed the station attendant, dropping coins on the bar. "I've had a belly full myself," he grunted, and stomped out into the sun.

Following the dust of the coach on his big stud was an easy task, and when a higher trail presented itself, Zac scampered the horses toward the higher ground, taking care not to skylight himself. His desire was to find targets, not become one.

The boulders rose up from the hills and scrub pine dotted the greasewood while the road stretched beneath his view. Zac knew the coach would stop at the creek below, and so he let the horses drink belly deep in it while he took in a good view of what lay ahead. The big stud seemed skittish and his nostrils flared after crossing the rushing high creek. The horses stomped and swung their heads to face upwind.

Then Zac spotted the bear tracks. Evidently, a large grizzly had been feeding on some berries by the creek bed a short time before.

The animals were anxious to be clear of the place and Zac was only too happy to oblige. They made good time on the trail that skirted the canyon wall, and soon he spotted a flat area that led out onto an overhang. Figuring this to be a likely place to get a good view of the road below and be able to observe anyone who might be lying in wait, Zac ground hitched the horses to some brush and, on his belly, inched up to the edge of the rocks with his binoculars.

The sun drenched the boulders below in a golden glow and they rose from the valley floor like the withers of a hundred buckskin ponies. Zac pulled his hat low to cut the glare and scanned the terrain for something out of place, anything that didn't belong.

The first snort from the horses turned his head. Squealing with jerks and tugs, the animals broke free and raised a cloud of dust galloping back down the trail. Zac scampered to his feet before he could spot the intruder, but in the back of his mind he knew what he would find. The grizzly looked to be about eight feet high and had stretched himself full length to feel empowered in the face of the human.

A roar went out of his snarling jaws, and, bringing his front paws down, the beast loped in Zac's direction. His Creedmore was strapped to the side of the big stud and on its way back down the hill. The agent's knowledge of bears told him it was best not to face a grizzly with a Bowie knife no matter what tall stories are heard, and the thought of his Colt with half loads brought no great amount of comfort nary-a-ways. He did the only thing he knew could be done. Leaping toward the hill, Zac began a run down the sharp incline that led to the bottom of the valley.

The thought of hidden rocks and cliffs held no greater horrors than the menace that was chasing him. Behind him Zac heard the bear's paws as they hit the dirt. Its heavy breathing was punctuated by panting and deafening roars. He knew enough about bears to know that many can and do run down a horse in a short distance. He also knew that trying to move up the side of a hill would only be to the advantage of the bear with its powerful rear legs. No, he was counting on the shorter front legs and a loss of stability on the part of the huge animal to lend him a hand. Provided this one didn't take Zac with him on the fall, running downhill seemed the only way out.

The agent was spinning out of control; his boots turned on the talus and skree rocks that spread over the slope. Shale and dust rose from the palms of his hands as Zac hit the side of the hill. With a roar, the bear bounced over the top of the tumbling man as they both barreled down the hill. When he hit level ground, Zac scrambled to his feet and quickly swirled his head about to find some stone tower that might be climbed to safety. There was none.

Reaching back to the lone story he knew about unarmed survival from a grizzly attack, Zac dropped to his knees. He worked himself quickly into a ball at the feet of the huge, growling bear. It was a trick an old man on the trail had sworn by. There was no other choice now, however. Tucking his head low, he laced his fingers behind his neck and tensed every muscle in is body.

A cannonball. Just an iron cannonball, he thought. His mind raced, and with each heartbeat his fingers tightened behind his neck.

The beast roared, then dropped to the ground beside the frightened agent. Zac's heart fluttered on the inside like a trapped bird in a bony cage. The bear's muzzle sniffed at Zac's neck and its bare teeth raked at the back of his ever tightening fingers.

Hot breath poured a foul odor of death over and around Zac's head. Bracing himself, with saliva or trickling blood oozing between his fingers, he waited for the feel of long claws or teeth knifing into his spine. The great beast just pushed on him with his nose, and then with powerful swats tried to turn him over.

The loose fringe on Zac's buckskin jacket tore off between the teeth of the bear as Zac teetered back and forth on his knees, trying desperately to keep from tumbling over and exposing his vitals. It was the wrong time to think it, but Zachary desperately hoped those stories were lessons on survival and not just some campfire tales.

CHAPTER 7

Bridger took the watch out of his vest pocket and pressed open the lid. Hours had gone by since he had left town for the railhead, and by now his grumbling stomach, the low sun, and his watch told him the day was long done. He had found out little or nothing about Me Che's brother. It was as if the boy had never existed. The line bosses and foreman knew of him but could give Bridger no information. They seemed to skitter away from his approach like so many fish in a tide pool.

He tied up his roan outside the manager's private car and swung his hips free of the saddle. The big butternut roan reached back and nipped at his rider's rump. It was not a friendly bite, but one that showed the animal's frustration at being ridden so far and standing around all day with a saddle on his back. Bridger's full frame necessitated that he ride the biggest, meanest studs he could find, and an occasional kick or bite was all a part of having good horseflesh under him. He boxed one of the ears of the big animal before he cinched his reins to the rail outside the car. "I'm just as ready for vittles and the hay as you are, knothead!"

He tipped his hat to the men who stood outside

the car and knocked on the red door. Without warning a booming voice roared, "Don't be a standing there, come on in, Sheriff."

The smooth aroma of expensive cigars filled the small car, and the sweet smoke clung to the lace curtains, long since yellowed by sunlight and dust. The manager stood and extended his hand. His head was a mass of mussed up red curls and his face looked unshaven by several days. His stocky frame protruded above the desk and showed a body that was shorter than Bridger's by about a foot, but one that had been hardened by many years of long hours on the rails.

"Sheriff, it is an honor to meet you, to be sure, sir. I thought ye might be a comin' in to see me. Me name is Ian O'Brien, and I'm the ramrod of this operation. Please, have a seat." As Bridger settled into a green overstuffed Duncan Fife, the big Irishman rounded his desk and pulled up an oak ladder chair. It creaked loudly as he leaned forward. "I'm hearing you have an interest in one of our missing coolies?"

Bridger twitched his mustache. "I have an investigation into the motive for an attempted murder."

"You're daft, Sheriff. There's no need to find any motive." A smile that descended into a sneer broke across the ruddy Irishman's face. "I was there that morning having me breakfast with the good captain. The she-witch just attacked him with a butcher knife. There's no accounting for the mind of these Chinese. As I see it, you're either wasting your time for nonsense or snooping about in matters that don't much concern you."

The big lawman's day had been a long one and in spite of the harsh tone of his host, he settled back into the settee, squashing the springs beneath his backside. His light blue eyes bored a hole into the big Irishman. "Mr. O'Brien, when *you* ask questions about other people's business, that's snooping. This star on my chest" — Bridger lifted up the edge of his sheriff's badge with his thumb — "means that when I ask them, it's my job."

"Very well then, Sheriff. We'll be about the activity of you wasting your time for nonsense. Ask your questions."

"Fine," Bridger replied. "Did you know this Chinese worker of yours?"

"Sheriff, I wouldn't know the man if he stepped on me foot, and how anyone, including their own selves, could tell one of them apart from another is beyond me poor imagination. They show up. They work. We feed them and pay them off. What they do after that is their own problem — and possibly yours, I suppose."

"Seems to be a good thing for the railroad they show up and work as hard as they do," Bridger replied. "With all the gold strikes in the Sierras, I'd think you'd be lucky to keep anybody hammering spikes."

O'Brien held up both palms and seemed to wave away any criticism. "I'm sure as not saying they don't work hard. They do, and with little complaint and not much notion to set out for some wild goose chase in the gold fields."

Bridger stroked his mustache. "Thought occurs to me that you'd be well advised to try to hold them as close-by as possible and keep them from leaving," he said.

"What are you suggesting, Sheriff?"

"I've recently become acquainted with the white powder, opium. Never had it anywhere about until the railroad and your workers came this far. From what I hear, you railroad boys keep them supplied, and, by doing so, wind up keeping much of the wages that are paid out to them."

The manager rose to his feet. "Now we get to the snooping part, Sheriff. I'm a businessman and if I can keep workers happy and turn a profit, then I'm happy. What they do with those pipes of theirs is a matter entirely up to them. Ian O'Brien will not be their priest, assuming they had a soul. They come, they work, they get paid, and what they do with the money is none of your concern or mine." The brutish Irishman raised his fist chest high and with his thumb tapped his chest to make a point. "No, I just find a need and meet it, like any other businessman."

"Seems like a nasty business to me, Mr. O'Brien. Selling your own workers misery."

"You take me wrong, Sheriff. I may make a little profit on the side, but around here we're in the business of building a railroad. We'll build it over, around, or through your town, and nothing will stop me or slow me down from doing just that — not you, not that badge, nor all the saints in glory. Right now you're in me way and keeping me away from me work. I won't be in your way and I expect you to stay out of mine. I also won't be wasting a single minute worrying about some Chinaman and his sleep powder. That's me final word on the matter. Now, if you'll excuse me, I've got a railroad to build."

The cushions sucked wind as Bridger got up and walked toward the door. Putting his hand on the brass knob, he turned and said, "O'Brien, I happen to be the sheriff of San Luis Obispo County. Your railroad is in my jurisdiction. These coolies, as you call them, are citizens hereabouts, same as the rest. If I have to, I'll be back every day and go through each part of your operation until I am satisfied. Frankly, I don't care if you like it or not."

Unbuttoning the sleeves on his shirt, the sheriff rolled them methodically up his forearms. Each word the big man spoke seemed like carefully tossed pebbles into the cool blue pools of the Irishman's eyes. Every inflection, every phrase, was born out of deliberate thought carefully aimed at the mind of the rail boss.

Leaning his face toward the big redhead, he said, "Seems to me I'd like to find out if this young worker of yours may have got in your way, and find out I will, be assured of that. I am going to do my job, and if it interferes with yours, you can be sure that you'll be the one losin' sleep over it, not me."

Turning to the door again, Bridger stopped and then whirled around, a smile pushing his blond mustache up at the corners. "Come to think of it, O'Brien, I would prefer it if you decided to get in my way. That would please me a lot. It surely would."

The sheriff took no guff from anybody, least of all an easterner who considered himself important. He knew the railroad was well connected in the state and that by comparison his sheriff's office was small potatoes. The attitude he sensed at the rail line bothered him, though, and played through his mind as he started back toward town.

Bridger's eyelids drooped. Fatigue was taking a toll on the big man, and his ride back was unusually careless. It was his habit to draw the reins up from time to time and swing his mount to the side to make a careful study of his back trail. On this night, however, his mind was pondering the facts of the case as he knew it. The trail was all too familiar and its well-worn turf added to his indifference.

The big butternut had his own mind on that evening, and with the breeze blowing from town and into his face, the roan only had a rubdown and some oats on his mind. As the miles back to town passed, Bridger's thoughts drifted dangerously, lost to the sound of the distant surf, which lulled horse and rider into a conscious sleep.

Had he paused to stop from time to time and surveyed the territory he had just passed through, he could have easily spotted the two riders who

had ridden out of the railhead some distance behind him. They occasionally sculpted themselves
against the starry night on the treeless grassy bluffs
overlooking the sea. The two of them were taking
a careful pace, making sure they wouldn't overtake or lose the big lawman, and one of them
clenched a lit cigarette between his teeth.

The moonlight was already cavorting on the
waters off Shell Beach as Bridger rode up the
ridge and looked down on the lights of San Luis.
What he wanted most was to be home by his fire
now, but there was one more place he had to go.
Pulling up outside the warehouse on the edge of
town, Bridger shortened up on the reins.

He wasn't going to let the big roan get another
crack at protesting a stop that didn't have a barn
attached to it, so he walked the horse to the front
of the double doors and picketed the animal to a
metal hasp. Reaching into his saddlebags, he
pulled out a metal hammer and pulled the nails
out of the hinge that held the lock to the door.
Pushing the large door ajar, he stepped inside and
lit a match.

The shadows of the warehouse seemed to
flicker with the flame and bounce off the bales
and barrels that were stacked inside the wooden
cavern. Bridger found a lantern hanging on a post
and put the dwindling match to the wick. His
eyes, once adjusted to the starless indoor night,
quickly identified the office, and he began a slow
meander around the stacks toward it.

Cases of spikes and nails, combined with what

looked to be a ton of dynamite, showed the old warehouse to be possibly the largest single bomb on the coast. He knew the place belonged to the railroad and they had proper use of such things, but he shuddered to think of what one match could do to a town.

As he pushed on the door, the lock split the doorjamb, splintering it open with a jerk. Bridger searched the room, found the desk containing bills of lading, and sifted through papers that showed the manifests of shipments to the railroad. He had the mind of neither a freighter nor a clerk, but, being a man of the frontier, he'd been taught to track and hunt by searching for something out of place, something that didn't belong.

Nothing in the papers seemed to fit that description, however. Names of ships were identified beside each collection of items, and bills of lading were compiled in readable disarray. Everything appeared in order, at least as far as he could tell. He put the paperwork back in piles and began to look forward to going home and getting into bed, even if it meant crawling in without supper.

When he turned to leave, he saw them — something that didn't appear to belong — a row of barrels under the table marked "whale oil." Something in the back of his mind registered a warning and flashed the mental picture of a missing piece to the puzzle. He hadn't seen anything on any of the lists about the barrels, but remembered Zac had told him he'd been bringing a shipment of the stuff in from the longboaters in Cambria on the day he was ambushed. Zac had been doing Race Talbot a favor by delivering Talbot's whale oil to the Chinese market, however, not to the railroad. It seemed odd to Bridger's thinking that similar barrels were here in the railroad's warehouse.

Couldn't be the same ones, he thought. Still, it did seem odd to him that they would be kept inside the office when there was room in the warehouse.

During Jeff's years as a trapper, he'd kept his hair by paying attention to what was out of place: A bird flying suddenly when it shouldn't, crickets who weren't chirping, and frogs who weren't croaking — all were signals of danger. Now, a simple shipment of oil in the wrong spot — a locked office instead of the warehouse — seemed very much out of place.

Scooting a barrel out from under the table, he took his knife and pried open the lid. As he looked down into it, the glossy surface reflected the flame of the lamp that he held high, but little else. On little more than a whim, he reached his hand just below the liquid surface and touched a soaked stack of bags.

He reached in and pulled out a tightly sewn sheep bladder of the same type he had seen the day before at the big yellow house. He shook the oil off the surface of the bag, opened up the tightly sewn end with his knife, and watched white powder sift to the floor. He dipped his finger into the white powder and touched his tongue with it. *Opium!* he thought. *My God, I've got 'em!*

He couldn't remember what he felt first, or if it was the sound of a footfall he heard behind his back, but the distinctive and sudden chill of cold iron — something that felt like the blunt end of an axe — slammed suddenly into the back of his head. The lights inside his mind seemed to burst into a Roman candle of pain, followed by the sound of his own skull giving way to the blow and slowly bouncing against the dirt floor. A spinning sensation enveloped his entire body, giving him a cold rush like falling into a well. Then all was black.

CHAPTER 8

The flies had begun to buzz around Zac's fingers, each one bringing a tickle to his pain. His grip only tightened, and he kept his knees firmly tucked into his chest while the grizzly continued trying to turn this stubborn lump of flesh into a meal with each repeated swat.

Zac's tactic had indeed taken the beast by surprise and made work for him out of what should have been no contest. Each continued sniff of the animal's wet nose was followed by grunts and an occasional ear-shattering roar. The animal seemed to detect life with each inhaled breath, frustrating him and adding to his fury. With desperate swats, the beast's razor-sharp claws tore through the buckskin jacket and into Zac's flesh. The beast ambled off occasionally, only to turn and rush at the helpless man shivering in a ball on the ground. Each charge was preceded by loud roars of defiant bravado. There was no match on earth for the Silver-Tip Grizzly.

Suddenly, as if by magic, the big bear turned his head. Zac could sense him sniffing at the breeze. Then the monster of the mountains simply turned and loped off upwind to inspect the curiosity of some newfound smell. He turned in Zac's direction once or twice and seemed to puff and grunt, registering his victory or perhaps making a mental note of where to return.

The bear had emerged victorious. The man was not moving. He could always come back and turn him over later. With that self-assurance, the beast turned his head and ambled south.

Staggering to his feet, Zac stumbled down the hill toward the stage road, bumbling and tripping as he made his way to the valley floor. Bewildered from the loss of blood, he kept on going, not stopping for long periods, but frequently pausing to catch his breath and change the bandages he had made for his hands and back. He had to do his best to get out of the range of the bear. Deep down, he didn't believe he'd survive another attack.

His shirt and the remains of the jacket had served to stop the bleeding. The blood had dried and caused the shirt to bond to his back, forming a stiffened hide of torn skin and cotton. He needed water and shelter. Shock had sent his head spinning, and the road at the foot of the mountain was a needed orientation.

He had been on the valley floor for a short time when he came upon a fresh set of tracks. Shod hooves cut across the stage tracks that had gone before them. Hours of labored walking finally brought him through Cajon Pass and out onto the high desert. As he climbed the rise in the road, he saw the aftermath of what his time lost to the bear had cost. The stage lay on its side, bathed in the light of the setting sun. The wheels were still and tied up to the boot was a saddled horse. Zac figured it to be the horse that had been weaving in and out of the stage tracks since the pass.

From his vantage point, he could see a lone, waistcoated rider. The man was stooping down, inspecting a pair of lifeless bodies sprawled on the high desert floor.

The sight in the distance made Zac go numb. These holdup men had never before killed someone during a robbery, and Zac wondered what had happened to change them. He sat down by a rock to take note of the situation and watch for a few moments before calling out to get the rider's attention, but before he could make up his mind, the dark-suited man mounted up and began to gallop across the valley, toward the northeast.

Flies had found Zac's bloody back. He swiped at them and painfully rose to his feet. Lurching forward, he plodded toward the helpless vehicle in the distance. At first glance, the place was a puzzle. The traces that held the team had been cut, allowing the horses to run free. The strongbox carrying the payroll indeed was gone, and the driver and shotgun messenger had been killed. They lay on their backs in the sun with multiple gunshot wounds.

The air was still and quiet; then all at once, Zac heard the sound of singing in the distance. Rounding the coach with his gun drawn, he saw the boy and his father. The youngster sat by the coach with the body of his father, stroking the man's hair. Zac stood there, speechless. He thought anything spoken would seem an intrusion on the boy's privacy. A gunshot wound was clearly visible in the man's chest. In the lad's left hand was an open gold pocket watch. The boy seemed to be lost in looking at the timepiece. Not wanting to disturb him, Zac began to move toward the sound of the singing.

"The Union forever, hurrah, boys, hurrah . . ." The sounds trailed off into laughter. "While we were marching through Georgia . . ." they continued to sing.

Zac plunged down the bank of the wash, gun still in hand, pointing it at the two men who were alongside the dry creek bed. They were the miners he had seen at the stage stop, and now they were roaring drunk. The sight of Zac with a gun in his hand, however, served to sober them up somewhat.

"Hey, who are you?" one of them shouted.

"Yeah, you can't take anything. We'ze done been robbed already," the other one said.

Zac holstered his pistol before walking over to the men and stooping down beside them. They each held a half-empty bottle of rye and were being quick about seeing the bottom. "You want to tell me what happened here?" Zac asked.

"Yeah. Ulp . . ." the first man burped out. "We wuz robbed."

"Yeah," the second miner spoke up, "a whole bunch of masked men stopped the stage and made us get out. Then they put us on foot."

"Yep, they cut the lines to the team and drove 'em off," the first one said.

"How were those men killed?" Zac asked.

"Oh, yeah. They asked for our watches and any jewelry we were carrying. Now, what man would carry jewelry?" The two drunks looked at each other and shook their heads. The first miner continued, "They did look at our watches, though. We thought they were gonna take 'em too, but they never did."

"Naw, I guess they jest wanted a look-see at 'em," said the other. "But that feller Bond didn't give 'em a chance. He said, 'I'll not give up my watch.' Said something about his wife giving it to him. That's when they shot him."

The first miner drunkenly slurred out, "They must have thought he was heeled, 'cause when he put his hand on his vest, they just let him have it."

"Yeah, then when the driver and messenger made a move for their weapons, they turned the guns on them boys too. It was a bloody mess, it was. I don't know what them boys had against that poor Mr. Bond though, him with a boy along and all, but they shot him, they surely did.

" 'Course, after all that, we handed over our timepieces right quick. They just looked at 'em and gave 'em back, never even opened 'em up. Now ain't that strange?" With that, the two men began to gulp down more of the "Who hit John," and Zac wandered back to the coach.

"Boy, don't be frightened. They're all gone

now," Zac said. He removed his hat and the scarf that had been matted with the blood from his own wounds and, pouring some water from a canteen into the handkerchief, began to wipe the brow of the frightened child. "Don't be afraid, boy."

Several minutes passed as Zac sat, quietly looking at the grieving boy. "You've been through a lot, son. You just set yourself here while I dig their graves, then we'll do some talkin'." Zac took the shovel out of the back of the coach and started to dig.

This was the kind of thing that haunted him. There was no explanation for this. It was cold-blooded murder. He wondered at the identity of the lone rider he'd seen earlier. *No casual passerby could stop at this scene and just ride off,* he thought.

The sun had set, and when he had finished burying the bodies, the faint light to the west coated the ground in a soft glow. The men were below coyote level when he patted down the mound on the last grave and pulled the boy up from beside the coach. "Son, we're gonna say a few words over your pa and these other gentlemen, then I got to go look for some horses and water."

Zac wasn't about to fetch the two miners for the occasion. The child had gone through enough without having those two drunks stumbling over his father's grave. He pressed the boy close to him and they walked to the last mound. "This here is where your pa is buried."

He noticed the watch the boy was holding, and stooping down, Zac looked at the picture that was in the open lid. It was of a beautiful dark-haired woman holding a baby. "I assume this is you and your ma." The boy nodded slightly, then seemed to squeeze the watch even tighter. "Here, boy, I've got somethin' to show you."

With that, he took his own watch out of his vest pocket and ran his fingers along the gold chain to the locket. Opening it, he showed the boy the picture of Jenny. "This here's a good friend of mine, boy, and she bakes some of the best apple pies you ever put in your mouth."

The boy looked at the picture and seemed to soften. Zac continued, "My folks are gone, too. 'Course, I was a mite older than you when it happened."

Zac tipped back his hat and seemed to stall for time. He knew no amount of words could help the boy, but it didn't stop him from searching for the right ones. "Just from what little I saw of your pa at that stage stop, I could tell he was a Christian gentleman, and if that's true then he's in heaven now with your ma."

Zac paused. "You know, at funerals, we're all sorry for ourselves. We say we're there to remember the people we're buryin', but we're really there for ourselves."

Zac paused as they both listened to the wind. "I read the Bible myself at one time. Goin' by what it says and what my mamma used to tell me, I'll just wager that right about now your pa's happier than he's ever been before." Zac looked down at the youngster and took off his hat. "Nothin' anybody says or does can ever bring them back. The only thing you and I can do from here on out is to make sure we're ready to go where they've gone. Now let's stand up and see that your pa gets a proper burial."

They stood by the grave, and Zac placed his hand on the boy's shoulder while the youngster continued to clutch the open watch. "Lord, we don't know what to say. We don't know, either one of us, why we're here alive and these good men are dead. All we know is that you're still God and we're still here."

The boy looked up at him with silent tears running down his cheeks. The words of many funerals floated into Zac's mind — words he'd swear he'd spent a lifetime listening to, words he'd spent just as long trying to forget. He looked into the boy's eyes. "Boy, I'm not much of a praying man, but I'll do my best. The Almighty is listenin', I know enough to know that. I know He even listens to us when there ain't no words comin' out."

Zac lifted his eyes to the pink clouds of the sunset. He took a few deep breaths, then glanced down to make sure the boy's eyes were off of him. Looking back to the sky, he began to pray again. "We know, Lord, that you've promised to come back and that when you do, this good man and all those others that have trusted in you will come back too." Zac fumbled for the words. "Until that happens we know that the Lord giveth and the Lord taketh away. Blessed be the name of the Lord."

With that, Zac put on his hat. "Boy, I've got to get movin' if I ever expect to catch those men who killed your pa. You could stay here and wait for help. When the coach is overdue tonight, they'll send some people to look for it. I just can't stay and wait for that to happen."

The boy stood ramrod straight and looked into Zac's eyes, pleading to go with him, though not saying a word.

Zac knew that the last thing he needed was a child tagging along, but there was something in this boy's look that cut him to the quick. It was like looking back into a mirror and seeing himself years ago. To walk away from this boy would be to walk away from everything his mother and father had ever taught him, everything he knew to be true.

"All right, I guess it's you and me. Right now we've got to get shuck of anythin' that will slow us down. I'll carry this Colt and one of the canteens and you carry the watch." The boy nodded.

Hours of walking had produced no horses and no water. Each step away from the road following the team led them into a wide circle to the east and up to the dry bed of the Mojave River. Darkness completely filled the sky now, and continuing to track the horses would prove fruitless. Zac scrambled down the bank and into a leeward bend of the bone-dry river. Scooping out sand, he began to dig.

"Boy, these rivers carry flash floods any time of year, so we can't make camp here. But they can also leave some water or at least wet sand below the surface, so let's dig and leastways wet our mouths."

Zac continued to dig while the boy sat watching him, stone cold and silent. In a short time darker sand appeared, then a pool of dirty water formed. Zac wet down his handkerchief and handed it to the boy. "Suck on this." He dug deeper and submerged his hat, drawing it out for a sandy drink for the boy first, then for himself.

They settled onto the bank of the old riverbed and quickly built a fire from the dried mesquite. Only the crackle of the wood broke the silence of the night. The stars overhead were bright and an occasional shooting star fell into the horizon. A low moon hung over the San Gabriels — an orange, bloody, lonely moon. There was no need to talk. The memory of the graves and the long walk hung around the edge of the campfire, separating the man and the boy from the rest of the world with a veil of emotion. They were two frightened wanderers of the desert, lost in a hostile world where greed had temporarily triumphed over goodness.

The boy stared into the flames as a cloud of sparks popped and rose into the indigo sky. Zac learned long ago when on picket duty in Virginia not to stare into the fire at night. It cut down on night vision and was dangerous if you had to look into the darkness for the enemy. He scrutinized the cool earth and began to draw in the sand with a stick.

He thought about the fact that he had been so cocksure of himself. "I'll be on that run," he had said to one person after another. "The payroll will get through," he'd bragged. Yeah, he'd been so clever trying to take the head of the operation off. Now, it was pretty obvious that whoever hit the stage did it with the intention of murdering him. Someone who'd gotten a good look at him in San Bernardino had given them something to look for — the locket on his watch. How could he have known that the man's watch was the one thing the boy's dad felt was worth fighting for? The robbery had cleared the stationmaster Bill Sampson, but . . . He looked at the boy, his cheeks dirty and tear-stained, and thought, *If it hadn't been for them wantin' me, the boy's father would be alive. He wouldn't be an orphan, like me.*

He turned to the child. "What's your name, boy?"

Blinking to hold back tears, he haltingly answered, "SSS . . . Skip, sir, but folks call me Sk . . . ss . . . skipper, Skip Bond. I ain't been able to ttt . . . talk so good sss . . . since my mmm . . . mother died."

Zac continued to draw on the ground. "Well, Skip Bond, you got yourself any people in California?"

The boy looked down and began to shake his

head even before speaking. "No, sir. D-D-Daddy and me's got a place near Ivanhoe. Mother died there . . . a c-c-couple of years back. We wuz in Los Angeles to claim some money from b-b . . . back East. My grandparents died and sent us some money. We put it in the b-b-bank."

The boy began to draw on the ground with his finger, imitating Zac's posture. He shifted his gaze toward the stars. "I reckon th-th . . . they're all up in heaven now."

Zac looked at the darkened sky. "I reckon so, Skipper. Meanwhile, we're here." The boy only slowly nodded, his blond, mop-like hair rising and falling.

The idea of having someone depending on him terrorized Zac. He had passed on his own happiness with Jenny just so he wouldn't have to account to anybody, wouldn't have to explain himself, wouldn't have to excuse himself. He had tried to live a straight life, but he sure didn't need anybody waiting around for him — not a wife, not a boy. Just now though, he felt mighty responsible.

Zac took the locket out of his pocket and opened it to the picture of Jenny, then looking over at the boy, he noticed the open watch in the lad's hands. *Two lonely orphans,* he thought.

The San Gabriel mountains in the distance had now settled into the blackness. Zac rose to his feet to stretch. It was then he heard the sound of a horse, accompanied by a muffled cough. He drew his Colt and, flattening down near the fire, threw sand on it to stifle the flames. "Come over here, Skip, and quick. Get down behind me."

The boy's breathing became heavier as he scrunched in close to Zac. He wound his arms around Zac's waist, thrust his head into the still painful back of the prone agent.

"Hello, the camp," a raspy call seemed to echo down the dry wash. "We seen your fire. We're comin' in."

Zac lifted his head to reply, "Walk in slow with your hands empty." The men fanned out as they approached the fire-circle, and before Zac saw their faces clearly, he spotted the speckled white rump of his Appaloosa. The man leading him was carrying a rifle.

"That be your voice, Mr. Gamblin' man? We'ze got your big bad rifle and your little shotgun here, but we ain't got no deck of cards."

It was the McKenneys!

CHAPTER 9

"Empty your hand," Zac called out in the dark.

The older man spoke slowly, "Naw, we ain't gonna be no worriation to ye boy, and you ain't gonna be no problem neither. I'd say with this here scatter-gun of your'n and the pistols we carry, we got aces high. Besides, we got your pretty horse to do some tradin' wif."

For the first time, Zac had more to worry about than how to snap off the quickest shots and try to roll clear of the return blasts. He had a frightened child hugging his waist. While they might miss him, they might not miss the boy. He tried to sound confident. "All right, step forward and let's talk."

"Now that would jes' be plain foolishness, wouldn't it, Mr. Gambler. Holdin' aces high like we is and then foldin' the pot. Naw, you jes' throw out that Colt pistol of your'n, then we'll come in, set a spell, and talk."

Zac didn't know if the McKenneys were behind the holdups, but he did know that if they were, they were here to kill him — kill him, and then the boy. He slowly took out his shopkeeper's model belly gun from beneath his belt. Reaching behind him, he handed the pistol to the child. "Skip, stick this in my belt back there," he whispered. He then raised the heavy Peacemaker to catch the firelight. "All right, here it is," he said. Tossing the Colt to the ground, he invited them into the campsite. "Come on in."

The older man walked into the camp, flanked by the two younger ones. "That there's a more peaceable attitude." The old man sat near the dying fire and began to stir the coals and add new wood.

"Now, I do believe we've got something that belongs to you. Came across this fine Appaloosa with all your gear still strapped on him today. Figured you'd run into some trouble." The boy began to peep over Zac's shoulder and his blond hair picked up the lights of the growing fire.

One of the younger men cracked a toothy smile. "Whoa, looky here, Pa. The licorice kid's here with the gambler."

The old man spoke, "Now what's a mean man like you doin' with this child?" With that he rose, and as he walked toward Zac, Skip quickly stuck the hideout gun into the rear of Zac's waistband. McKenney reached over Zac and hoisted the boy by his pants, taking him over to the fire. Cobb froze with the prospect that what he might do could endanger the boy.

Zac got to his feet and put his hands on his hips. "You steal from a child, then rough him up to boot, do you? That boy's been through hell today. His father's out buried by the coach along with the driver and shotgun messenger on that run, and I'll not have him suffer any more. Let's have you drop him and try someone who's your own size." The McKenneys were stocky, muscular men, their bulk revealing little or no fat.

The old man put up his hand. "Don't get riled up, now. We aim you no harm. Sure, we found your horse, one of 'em leastways, and we seen the coach. Saw them graves you dug and started to trail you till night fell. If it hadn't been for your fire, we like to never found you."

"I wouldn't have lit it, if it hadn't been for the boy."

McKenney lowered the boy near the fire, but the child scrambled to his feet and ran back to wrap his arms around one of Zac's legs.

Pointing to the boy, the old man spoke. "I surely do admire a child with spunk. Hope this here day's trouble don't cut him back too much, surely do. Name's Jock McKenney. These here are my boys, Jack and John. We got us a mine up in San Grigonio area. We don't hunt no trouble, jes' let off a little steam now and then. We were feelin' our oats and kinda proddin' trouble back there at the stage stop."

Looking down at the boy clinging to the agent's leg, the old man scratched his beard and, with hands on his knees, lowered his head to stare into the child's wide eyes. "Feel mighty poorly about your pa, boy. Sure do. He made us feel powerful bad in that station house. Couldn't hardly look each other in the eye after your stage left. We decided after that to go on up to Calico and gamble. We wuz also hopin' to find you, boy."

He turned to his youngest dark-eyed son. "John," he said.

The dirtiest of the trio reached into his pocket and produced a shining silver dollar. He tossed it into the sand in front of the boy. "Sorry," he said.

The old man looked at the boy. "I come out here in '48, and what your pa said about money reminded me of my own mother, and some of the things my wife used to say about my gold huntin' all the time. They were women of beliefs. Dang sure took me back. Your pa was a good man, boy."

The remainder of the evening was spent cooking pemmican in the canteen water carried by the horses. Made of buffalo stock, it cooked up like beef stew, and the warmth of it took the chill out of the desert. Talk of the robbery and the description of the condition of the coach and passengers was enough to make the most hardened man shudder and scratch his head.

Later, when the supper things were put away, smiles broke out all around when Zac reached into the saddlebags and produced a deck of cards.

Daylight was a ways off when Zac started pounding the coffee beans in his frying pan with the butt of his Peacemaker. They turned the foam of the boiling water a soft brown when he threw them in. He was slicing bacon to fry when the oldest McKenney boy, Jack, walked up. "You goin' after them holdup men, ain't you?" Zac nodded and continued to slice the meat, laying it in the frying pan. The young man stooped beside him. "You must be some kinda bounty hunter, then."

Zac shot a look in his direction and said, "Just of a sort."

The boy continued to make conversation. "I knew you were, 'cause you got yourself some sand. I took one look at that Sharps rifle with all them sights and knew what you wuz. That is some kind of weapon."

Zac spread apart the sizzling bacon and settled back on his haunches. "Well, I tell you; I couldn't lug around a rifled cannon, so that has to do. I do believe, though, that if I'd a had that piece during the war, things might have been different. But I didn't and it wasn't."

The aroma of the brewing coffee and frying bacon began to arouse the rest of the camp, and the older McKenney boy inhaled the scented smoke and wiped his nose with his dirty sleeve. "I figure you're gonna need some powerful help in catchin' them fellers. Especially if they're the ones that been doin' all these holdups. We're miners, you know, and when there's problems in the mines we all feel the blow. Why, I heard tell some of the big minin' boys in Calico wuz plannin' on haulin' their own payrolls to town and hiring special guards."

Zac lay the crisp bacon on a wide rock near the fire. He looked up at the young man and commenced to speculate as if thinking out loud, "I don't imagine Wells Fargo will take too kindly to losing their business. 'Course they're giving it up now . . ." He stopped and looked into the young man's face. ". . . one strongbox at a time." His voice rose and he spoke directly to the young man, "My plans are to get back to that coach and begin trackin' those men." His words seemed so matter-of-fact. "I'll find them, and then I'll kill them."

Zac kept his back to the young man as he poured a cup of coffee. Facing him, he handed it to him, handle first. Taking another cup, he poured one for himself, then stared into the glowing coals as the dawn began to crest over the Mojave like a pink ribbon topping the blue desert mountains.

"What you gonna do with the young boy?" The question from the young man brought no response, only a distant look from Zac in the direction of the coming dawn.

As they rode west through the Mojave, the day stretched out with the small talk of two strangers learning each other's patterns. Zac began to ease his reflexes, and the strange feeling of small arms wrapped around his waist became a more welcome comfort. *A man has no future until he can pass on his life through somebody else,* he thought. *Without that, the present is hollow and not fully lived.*

Midmorning, he cut the trail of the lone rider who had stopped at the coach the day before. The fact that the man had stopped and then ridden on had been buzzing about in Zac's head all night. The sharp edges of the tracks showed a man in a hurry, and Zac figured him to be someone who knew where he was going.

The gang who had held up the stage would be riding circles through the roughest country and hardest rocks they could find. They knew the territory and had a plan for escape already laid out, but whoever the fella was who had followed them was not expecting to be trailed.

All the trouble the agent would go through to find a man with a sixteen-hour start on him, however, would go for nothing unless the lone rider was connected to the holdup men. They had left the holdup site in the opposite direction, but Zac was counting on them all ending up in the same place, at which point he would join their trail.

Zac stopped the Appaloosa near the bottom of a rise and circled a ridge that would have sky-lighted him. The tracks he followed led over the same hill in full target view of anyone with a gun. He reined the stud around, choosing instead to meander through a wash. As they penetrated the other side of the wash, a dry lake bed stretched out below them, its white sand broken by only one set of tracks. Whoever was ahead of him, Zac figured, was either innocent or ignorant.

The sun of the Mojave began to pour out its wrath long before it was directly overhead. The bare boulders of the desert floor squinted in the sun. There were no shadows, only parched rock.

These were bleached bones pushed along by the great river of long ago, a river long since dry. Zac and Skip rode the Appaloosa across the lake bed. They stopped at the edge of the flat in the beating sun to take a liberal drink from their canteen.

"Skipper, take a big drink, but swallow it slow. We got no time to wait for sundown, otherwise we'd cross this stretch at night. This place is like hell with the fire put out." The boy caressed the huge canteen, and with two hands held it to his parched lips, savoring each sip. "When you're in the desert, Skip, you gotta drink what you have. To spare it is to let the heat take your brains away. Do that and you'll have yourself wanderin' in the wrong direction and makin' no sense at all, while you're nursin' a full canteen." Zac poured some water into his peaked hat and allowed the stud to slurp up what was there with his pink, darting tongue.

The ground began to break up into pointed rocks of sharp obsidian and porous but flat out-croppings. They dismounted to better pick their way through the maze, and Zac began to follow the general direction of the tracks without staying on top of them. The distant hills were showing more definition, and a shimmer of heat rippled through the air before them. Zac picked up two pebbles from the ground and tossed one to the boy. "Skipper, roll this around in your mouth. It'll cut your thirst some and keep the moisture in your mouth movin'."

They mounted and were still keeping pace with

the tracks that showed no sign of concern that someone might be following. The low, dull sheets of rock that would have lent themselves to a change of direction were habitually stepped around and over. Floors of rock were entered, only to show tracks on the other side in the same direction that the rocky shelf had been penetrated.

They mounted the stud and began to close the distance, following the clear trail of fresh, overturned dirt that had been their guide. The big Appaloosa was over sixteen hands high, and even with the extra weight, he made good time and never seemed to tire.

Nearing a shelf of white boulders, they spotted a drop into a small valley offering some shade. The first of the greasewood bent into gnarled tangles and caught the boy's shirt as they turned to meander down the hill. Turning to pull the shirt loose from its captor, Zac spotted the sentry. He sat under an overhang halfway around the valley, not fifty yards away. His legs were stretched out before him and his arms were folded around a rifle. His body looked to be totally relaxed, with a hat pulled down over his eyes to offer what shade could be found on the hillside.

Zac put up his finger to the boy's eyes and pointed out the relaxed picket; gently, he pulled the snagged shirt from the branch, taking care not to snap a twig or make a noise that might arouse the unconscious observer across the way. Only the guard's siesta had prevented them from being seen. They quietly dismounted and, with Zac's hand on the Appaloosa's muzzle, swung around the boulders at the rim of the canyon. What they had to do would wait until nightfall.

CHAPTER 10

The evening stretched out softly over the desert floor; like a dark giant unfolding his gangly legs after a hard day's work, it pushed its way under rocks and over the top of the dry lake bed. Wildlife had begun to scurry about in search of food and water, and in the distance a flock of vultures soared over something that had failed to survive the heat of the day.

The stud cropped a growth of scrub, and Zac worked hard at cleaning and reloading his weapons. Making sure the dust of the day wouldn't impede the smooth action of his revolvers was a must. With each manipulation of the oiled cloth over the blue steel, he quietly talked to the yellow-haired boy, who sat close by his side with eyes that drank in each adjustment, and ears that fixed themselves to the manly lessons of gunsmithing.

"Skipper, each day is hard enough to survive in the desert, and before you might have to use your firearms, you've got to make sure the desert hasn't been too hard on them. Wind-blown sand is no friend to a firearm, for example." He smoothly turned the cylinder of the Peacemaker and rubbed down the hammer. "Each one of these arms makes a healthy noise all its own.

When you hear it, you know it's ready."

The boy drank in every word of the man who had become his protector and mentor. Zac clearly recalled his own boyhood on a farm. The hoe and the plow had been what boys learned to handle. Guns and such were the magical world of after work, and work never seemed to end.

To his father and grandfather, guns were more necessary; the Cherokee and Seminoles made sure of that. For Zac, however, growing up in the red clay of Georgia had held very little adventure and mostly hard work. The coon hunt on a Friday night was the excitement of the week. The dogs ran them, and the men chased and shot them, their eyes twinkling in the torchlight from the top of the tree. Zac's job was to fetch them and skin them, till he was about seven or eight.

He could remember the first night he was allowed to shoot. His father had steadied his arm and spoken into his ear. He said, "All right, little buddy, your trigger's all set. You jes' follow that coon's eyes back a little and put a light touch on that second trigger there." The big muzzle loader roared and the sound of the coon falling through the branches of the tree had been music to his ears. One less varmint to steal chicken eggs, as far as the men were concerned, but a trophy of manhood to Zachary Taylor Cobb.

"Skipper, I'm gonna leave you here with the horse. We're far enough away from the draw so you won't be seen. Just keep quiet." Zac reached up to the saddle and unhooked the flour sack tied to the pommel. He took out the sawed-off ten-gauge and, breaking it open, handed it to the boy. "Boy, this is your equalizer tonight. With this you're as old as anybody seven feet tall and three hundred pounds. But be very careful with it."

Zac removed the shells, then closed the gun and handed it to the young boy. "Try cockin' the hammer and pullin' the trigger. Normally, I'd never let someone dry-shoot a weapon, but I just want you to get the feel of how the trigger pulls."

The youngster used both hands to set each hammer back and powerfully pulled the trigger, producing a sharp metallic rap with the descent of each hammer. Several attempts brought about the same successful results.

They quietly unhitched the stud and walked another hundred yards down the ridge, where Zac had spotted some unusual cover. The dark hole was deceptive from the outside looking in. It was a lava tube of frozen heat, long congealed into a tunnel that broadened into a dark cave. The floor, walls, and ceiling of the cave were all formed from the same porous black rock that had littered the desert floor — sharp spiny rock, good for nothing but concealment and pain.

Zac pushed the Appaloosa farther back into the cave and, hobbling the horse, stationed Skip near the entrance. "Skipper, this is your post. We don't know who the men are down there, but I'm gonna injun up to the cabin and try to look 'em over. When I get back, I'll whistle a little birdcall before I come in."

Zac loaded the young boy's weapon, dropping a shell into each chamber and slamming it shut. "Boy, this is about the most dangerous close-in weapon a body can use. Don't cock the hammers until you intend to use it, and when you do, make sure they're up so close they can't be missed." The towhead nodded and his hands clinched a death-lock on the little blunderbuss. "Don't aim the gun. Keep the butt of it against this here wall, then point it and pull one trigger."

Zac turned to go, then stopped and stooped to put his hand around the boy's neck and pull him closer. "We don't know for sure who these men are. We didn't follow the group that killed your pa, so we want to make sure. This is as safe a place as any. You've got the big Ap behind you and he'll tell you if anythin' isn't like it oughta be."

Skip's eyes glistened in the starlight of the cave opening as he walked with Zac out into the open air. "MMM . . . Mister Cobb . . . please don't get hurt."

Zac turned and moved along the desert's edge toward the opening to the canyon below. Perhaps he had lived life a little too foolhardy. He had had little to concern himself with, except his own hide. Distractions were something he had thought he never needed. They were only something that would cloud his thinking at the wrong time, something that would slow him down with the thought of self-preservation when he had a job to do.

He had thought he needed no one to interfere with his ability to plan, no one to make him hunt for cover when he should be steadying his aim for a second shot. Now the thought of a little boy in the desert, which his plan had helped to orphan, tore up his insides. His basic sense of fairness wouldn't let him die. Not tonight. Not now.

As he crouched by the greasewood tree where Skip had snared his shirt, he paused to look to the posted sentry's last position. There he was! Not fifty yards away a cigarette glowed in the dark. He was there, and he was not asleep!

Zac's hands felt for the wall of the canyon as he inched his way down the trail to its floor. The door to the stone cabin was cracked open, allowing the night air to cool the inside, and light leaked out of the edges along with loud voices.

Zac stepped carefully along the ground, avoiding any branches or rocks. All the while, he continued to occasionally glance upward, strangely comforted to see the glowing cigarette tip. Each time it grew bright, Zac knew the sentry was taking a puff and not paying close attention. Zac's hands felt for the rocky handles of the wall as each boot searched for a new perch. He loosened the tong on the hammer of his Peacemaker and his tensed muscles seemed to cause the minutes to drag by.

He found himself not thirty yards away from the cabin when the door was kicked open and light streamed out of its opening. The instant deluge of lantern light caught Zac's position and glued him to the canyon wall along the trail. The fresh light had also simultaneously sent a jack rabbit bolting from some brush near him, with pebbles kicked up by the rabbit actually landing near his boot. The rabbit went tearing across the canyon floor. Pressing his body against the rock, Zac moved his right hand quickly to the butt of his gun, holding it in place. He froze, fearing to breathe.

The man who had emerged on the porch made a quick movement for his six-gun, but seeing the rabbit, he relaxed and began to stretch his arms, taking in the night air. His frame was tall and slender, and he twirled the scarecrow-like arms that hung from his frame like a jay descending on a piece of bread, circling them to either side of his body. Zac remained motionless, hoping the scarecrow wouldn't follow the light up the canyon wall and onto his frozen position.

Moments later, the night intruder turned and, walking back into the cabin, closed the door. Zac turned and, lifting his head, searched for the ever-present glow of the cigarette on the ledge. It was gone!

He moved quickly down the hard, rocky slope as the horses in the corral began to stamp their hooves. They were still saddled, and he gathered they had been ridden only hours before he arrived that afternoon. They began to bluster and whistle with a shrill sound from their throats, one that indicated the approach of a stranger. To anybody with sense, a horse was better than a watchdog;

with its good hearing and keen sense of smell, it could pick out an intruder long before a human being could.

Paying close attention to the light around the door and windows, Zac held his hand out to one of the horses, while the rest of the remuda moved nervously around the pole ring.

He listened closely to the loud voices and pressed his eyes to the slits in the shutters that covered the window. He could make out a seated figure in a dark waistcoat with his back to the window. He was obviously the one Zac had trailed through the day. Three or four other men sat around the table raking gold coins into leather bags, while a much larger man with a burly black beard was leaning across the table, making intense eye contact with the man in the black coat.

The big man with the black beard wore a large revolver across his waist. His black eyes flashed from under heavy, brush-like eyebrows that came together in a solid black line across his forehead. Around the band of his hat, he sported a row of bear claws.

Zac had become much too familiar with the look of those deadly decorations and still felt the burning in his back from his lacerated skin. He watched the spittle fly from the big man's mouth as he croaked out his complaint to the man in the chair.

"We got that extra gold a comin' to us. We gone and done just what you said, only nobody would own up to it, so we killed that man just to make certain. It'll only insure that next time we draw down on a coach, them boys will stop and throw the box down all the quicker. Nobody makes me quit — not the law, not some bounty-huntin' Wells Fargo agent, not even you. If a mistake was made, it was yours. Right now, you're making another."

The man in the black coat spoke, but in a low tone Zac couldn't understand. Mr. "Bear Claws" apparently could, though, and the answer he got infuriated him even more. He rapped a silver-handled quirt on his chaps and his raspy voice rose.

"Us boys will continue to hit those coaches with or without your information. Who knows, maybe we'll get a bigger haul. Only this time, we won't be making any split with you. We take the risks, not you! They'll be tryin' mighty hard to see us swing whilst you sit in your office or in some cantina." He stopped his tirade and paced back to the opposite side of the cabin; turning with his hands on his hips to face his seated opponent, he exploded, "One man! One stinkin' man! Why all this trouble over one man?"

Zac began to count the number of men in the room. There appeared to be six, including the man in the black coat. He needed a better view, though, to make sure he wasn't missing someone perched on the wall nearest his window vantage point. He also wanted to get a good look at the face of the man in the black coat. He began to circle to his left, moving behind the cabin to see if another window might offer a better slant on what he was up against. His objective was clear — get rid of them, kill them all, before they killed somebody else.

"What the . . . ?" A thin, gangly man with a rifle ran smack into Zac as he rounded the corner of the cabin. It was the sentry, and Zac knew his time was up. Zac held on to the man as he yelled and began to struggle.

The rifle exploded in the air. The flame of the muzzle blast arched into the darkness as Zac reached across his belt and extracted his large Greener knife. Instantly they slammed together into the rear rock wall of the cabin, Zac bringing the knife up with his fist into the man's upper belly below the rib cage. Killing a man face-to-face brings home the horror of death. The man stood pinned to the wall at the end of Zac's arm. His eyes bulged slightly and seemed to stare into eternity while the air left his body in a muffled "huumppf."

Zac let his surprised foe slide off the end of the knife, and then looked around quickly before making a running dive for a set of boulders that dotted the back of the cabin. The door sprung open and the men inside had begun to douse the lamps and swing open the shutters.

As Zac ran for cover, he could hear the loud voices and running footsteps of the men on the front porch of the cabin and heard the song of a bullet as it sailed past him, evidently fired from the rear window. Diving into the dirt behind the rocks, Zac lay for a moment, catching his breath and listening to the banging of his heart.

He heard the men yell when they came upon the body of the sentry. They continued firing and he could hear movement in the horse corral. When the firing from the house stopped clipping at the rocks around him, Zac heard the pounding of the horse's hooves as they galloped up the canyon trail. He couldn't figure out why the gang had lit out so quickly, unless they were afraid he'd brought a posse with him, or unless they figured there was one close behind. Few men would dare work alone on a bunch this size, but that was how Zac preferred it. *Maybe they had something else to protect,* Zac thought. *The loot from the robbery, for instance.*

There was nothing more to be done here than look for whatever clues he might find. He needed to know where these men were headed and get some idea about who they were, especially the one in the black coat. He cautiously moved to the corral, where two horses had been left by the fleeing bandits. He assumed one of the mounts had belonged to the sentry and could only guess who might ride the other. It did give him pause for thought. He lightly put his footfall on the steps of the cabin. If anyone had been left behind to see to him, he wasn't going to walk into it, like the sentry out back had walked into him.

With the muzzle of his Peacemaker, he pushed open the door. It gave way with a creak of unoiled hinges that sent a shiver up Zac's spine as he stared into the darkened room. The starlight would only serve to outline him in the doorway. As he began to inch into the door, two loud reports from a distant gun brought him up short. "Boom! . . . Boom!" It was the sound of his Meteor ten-gauge.

CHAPTER 11

Zac hurriedly mounted one of the saddled horses in the corral. He gave little thought to the owner of the other horse, assuming only that whoever it was had been left behind to take care of him. Scooping up the reins of the second horse, he took one last look at the darkened cabin and yelled, "Long walk back." As he turned the horses up the trail beside the canyon wall, he paused and drew his Colt.

The mounts stamped on the rocky ground, and in a matter of seconds a figure appeared in the darkened doorway. Only the lights from the night sky gleaming across a rifle barrel gave away the hidden gunman. Zac cocked and fired three well-placed shots into the darkened doorway, shots that were followed by the sound of the rifle falling on the wooden porch. Zac turned the horses up the canyon and scrambled them up the incline and onto the upper desert floor.

Within a matter of minutes, he was reining his newfound ponies up to the entrance of the lava tubes where he had left the boy. He had given little thought to the possibility of another ambush, and the notion of this oversight spooked him a little. The desert night wind had begun sailing past the entrance to the cave and dust accompanied the whistling of its ebony edges. The boy was heavily on his mind. Being afraid for someone else was a strange feeling for Zac. Right now, though, the boy was unfinished business, and Zac never liked unfinished business.

"Skip! Skipper! It's me, boy. I'm comin' in." He began to slowly inch his body into the cave; the wind blowing behind his back and the chill of what he might or might not find made his hair stand on end. Each slide of his boots along the darkened cave floor was muffled by the shrill moan of the wind across the entrance of the cave.

Just in case the boy was not the only one in the cave, assuming he was still there, Zac lit no match and made no further sound to give away his position. Before he reached the spot where he had left the boy, his boot touched a soft, large object that blocked his path. Zac stooped down. It was a body! And it was still warm. The man's sidearm was still holstered. Zac figured the fella must have been quite surprised by the double-aught greeting. Feeling along the ground, he found the shotgun just beyond the body, the barrel still hot.

With his small shopkeeper in hand, Zac stepped over the inert figure and began to crouch low, crawling forward on all fours. Within a few more yards the whine of the outside wind had a diminished effect on his ears, and he began to hear other noises coming from deeper in the cave. He heard a quiet weeping and sniffling. There was also the sound of hooves. Carefully, Zac moved to the side of the lava wall and, crouching down behind an outcropping, he pulled a match from his shirt pocket.

With his right hand, he sighted down the short barrel into the darkness while his left arm extended the match away from his body. He wanted to make sure that when he popped life to the match, he didn't make himself too prime a target. He raked his thumbnail over the sulfur tip and the spark shot into a small flame.

There he was! Sitting on a box, the boy was crying, with his head in his hands. Behind him stood the Appaloosa. The big horse swung his head around and the match light reflected a glare from the animal's eyes.

Zac dropped the match and, lighting another, reached into his jacket pocket for a candle stub. For a long while he said nothing. He just sat beside the boy, listening to the sobs and watching the tears drop from the youngster's face to his hands and then to the floor.

The touch of Zac's strong arm around the boy's shoulder produced a series of jerky, stuttering statements, alternating between sobs. "I d-d-d . . . didn't wa-wa-want t-t-t . . . to do it." The boy spat out the words while tears rolled down his cheeks. "W-W-W . . . Why d-d-d . . . didn't h-h-h . . . he stop?" The boy's shoulders shook with every breath. The thought of the already traumatized boy sitting even for a few minutes in a darkened cave with the corpse of a man he had just killed made Zac shudder as well. The boy had done what he was taught to do. Then he had moved to the back of the darkened cave, more frightened of what he couldn't see than anything. The agent who had faced and dispensed death on many occasions felt a growing respect for this tender young man.

"Son, you only did what you had to do." At the sound of his own family term for the boy, Zac's heart felt strangely but fearfully warmed. It made him feel protective, responsible.

The boy's eyes turned to him, and he asked, "W-W-W . . . Why d-d-d . . . didn't he believe me? I t-t-t . . . told him I'd shoot."

"Skipper, men who can't be trusted never learn to trust. You shot a thief and a murderer. Those kind are without conscience. When you can't love, you can't be loved. You just die alone, having never really lived." Zac wasn't sure if his speech had been more directed at the boy or himself, but the notion of him teaching trust and love to anybody was, on the surface, absurd.

Then Zac noticed the green box the boy was sitting on. It was marked with black lettering that read, "Wells Fargo."

"Let's have a look at that box you're sittin' on, Skip. You were well enough out of the way. To be sure, that fella wasn't comin' here lookin' for *you.*"

The boy stood, and Zac took his Bowie knife and pried the nails that held the hasp lock, then shook the brass fixture to the floor. Tilting the lid, he held the candle over the box, and the light fell upon stacks of new greenbacks. "Whoo, whee! There must be thousands of dollars here, boy. I'm guessin' it's the better part of quite a number of the holdups these boys have pulled."

At that moment, Zac was more interested in distracting the boy from the killing than in the money itself. The bank notes were wrapped in bands that identified the Mercantile Bank. "Son, the reward money alone for this will be sizeable, and I'm guessin' that since you was sittin' on it, it'll have to go to you."

He broke the candle stub in half, and leaving one lit with the boy, he lit the other half and went back near the entrance of the cave to take stock of the body of the unwelcome visitor. The dark coat vest was matted with blood, but there was no mistaking the fresh corpse. It was Jonas Patterson, the president of the Mercantile Bank! His pockets were stuffed with bills from the robbery. To steal from one's own bank, and have Wells Fargo pay the freight, was an easy way to quick money without having to dig in the hills for it. The brief impression Zac had formed of the banker led him to believe that there was a more power-driven motive to the heists than the money alone. Rifling through the man's coat pockets produced a telegram addressed to J. Patterson. It read:

Wells Fargo Agent, Zachary Cobb. Known to be dangerous to operation. Eliminate at all cost. Identify by badge under coat. Also carrying gold heart-shaped locket.

Signed. I.O./ SLO

The message disturbed Zac greatly. The thought that someone had wired ahead to expose his identity was enough to anger him, but the locket! Only Jenny knew about that. And he knew no one by the initials I.O. But, evidently, it was someone who knew how to identify him, someone from San Luis Obispo — someone who also knew about the locket.

The men on the coach had all been killed because someone was trying to make sure *he* was dead. The gang he had uncovered tonight had asked for the passengers' watches — not to steal them, but to identify him, and kill him. They had been specifically sent to look for a badge and a locket, the one Jenny had given him.

The night camp in the cave was passed without a fire. Zac huddled with the child and laid awake the rest of the night. He was afraid the members of the gang might come back when Patterson didn't show. He also worked on how someone in San Luis could be connected with this bunch. He found it hard to imagine that anyone from as far away as San Luis would be involved with robberies in the Mojave.

The sea captain had to be the only link. The man was allied with the railroad, that was certain, but how could the railroad be involved with a gang of thieves? Of course, these thieves stuck to stagecoaches. They were targeting Wells Fargo!

He was also concerned that if the lid was too far off of his cover, it would make his job or the prospect of continuing to live in the area that much more difficult.

He stuffed the telegram into his shirt pocket. He would say nothing to the boy. Not that it didn't concern him. It was now as plain as could be that he was the one responsible for little Skip's pain.

They made quite a sight riding into Calico the next day — Zac and the boy on one horse, and the body of the bank president tied hand to foot under the girth of the other. People stopped and stared at the horseback hearse, trying to place one of the three. As they passed the Busted Flush saloon, Zac noticed the horses they had trailed during the day, still saddled and ridden hard. Bad way to treat horseflesh.

He nodded at the exhausted string of horses as they passed and said to Skip, "The men who rode those horses treat 'em like 'Paches would. Desert Indians like the Apache have no great affection for horses; they ride 'em to death, eat 'em, then steal some more."

They leaned forward in the saddle as the horses pulled their way up the steep, dusty street. Zac had always been a flatlander, but these mining towns were built so steeply on the slopes that whatever didn't burn down fell down. Pulling up outside the marshal's office, Zac hitched the horses. Word was beginning to spread, and men came to peer out of shop doors and the batwing doors of saloons, including those of the Busted Flush.

Opening the door to the marshal's office, the two of them stood staring at a gray-headed man in a black suit, white shirt, and tie. His mustache drooped around a cigar, and he scribbled at forms that lay scattered around the desk. Zac took the heavy box that he had bound with ropes and sat it down beside the desk. As the lawman leaned back in his chair, Zac produced his Special Agent badge.

"Name's Zachary Cobb. This here is Skip Bond. His daddy was killed on the San Berdov stage that got held up."

The older man suddenly got to his feet. "That was a bad one!" He looked at the child. "Youngun, we been looking for you everywhere. I'm real sorry about your pa."

"He's been with me," Zac said. "I wasn't about to leave him overnight in the care of two drunks."

The marshal nodded his head and his eyes widened when he saw the box. "Did you catch 'em?" he asked.

"Not all of them," Zac replied. "I got the ringleader tied down on his horse outside."

The marshal's eyes flared.

"He's past carin'," Zac said. "The box here contains what's left of the loot and most likely some money taken from earlier robberies."

The old man blinked while he puffed a cloud of black smoke over his desk.

Zac went on, "I been trailin' the rest of the holdup men here, and think I spotted their horses tied up outside the Busted Flush when we rode in."

With that last bit of news, the glowing butt of the marshal's cigar dropped to the desk. He pounded out the sparks on his paperwork with his fist and proceeded to mumble under his breath. "Carn sarn it." Looking up at Zac and Skip, he went on, "You couldn't have brung me better news and worse news at the same time if you'd tried. I just got back from them graves on the road, and me and a posse been looking all around the brush fer two days fer the tramps that done it. There ain't a man in this town that wouldn't string 'em up on sight if he knew they wuz here."

He scratched his chin and looked apprehensive. " 'Course, most of the good men in town are either down at the bottom of a mine shaft this time of day, or still beating the bushes for the men you say you trailed here. How many you say there are?"

"I'd say we're lookin' at about four or five, all pretty desperate hombres."

"Well, that's a might lot for what I can count on just now. It could take me a while to get enough men to handle this."

Zac reached into his saddlebags and produced a holster and the shopkeeper Colt. Removing his vest, he slung the holster around his left arm, tying the end to his belt. He pulled on what was left of his tattered buckskin jacket to try to conceal his revolver. "You'd better move fast, Marshal. Totin' in a freshly shot body has always attracted attention in a town, and if those men don't know I'm here by now, they will shortly. You'll need me to point them out too. I'm gonna take this money to the Wells Fargo office and send a wire to the sheriff of San Luis Obispo. Can you deputize a few men and meet me at the Busted Flush in fifteen minutes?"

The marshal took a shotgun off the rack and broke it down to load. "Mister Cobb, I'd be right surprised if I couldn't get the entire town to bring rocks and stone these hombres. Men around here are mighty tired of going without, just so some no-count saddle tramp can spend freely. They're mighty riled. Fact is, you jes' might have to stay on to help me keep 'em incarcerated for the trial."

Zac spent the next ten minutes briefing the agent in charge at the Wells Fargo office and putting the loot safely away before the mine owners could come to claim their long-awaited payrolls. The boy's eyes bored into him each time Zac turned to look his direction. The youngster sat still in the office straight-back chair and watched transactions take place he knew nothing about. No word, no complaint about lack of food, even though Zac himself was a little hungry. The boy just seemed to sit wondering what was to become of him and listening to any word that might tip him off as to his fate.

Zac packed his briar pipe and lit the bowl. He

drew the smoke to his lips and blew it to the ceiling. He was growing impatient as he looked across the street to the saloon. Checking his watch, he walked to the door to leave. He had forgotten that Skip was now following him everywhere he went. As he opened the door, the music of the bell that dangled from the top of the door, one designed to alert the attendant to a customer, stopped Zac and Skip in their tracks. The boy's eyes rose to look at the dangling brass music-maker.

Zac looked down at the lad's shining face and turned back to the agent at the counter. "This here is Skip Bond. He's from Ivanhoe, up near Visalia; was on the coach, the only survivor. He's also the one who found the stolen money, so the reward is his."

Stooping down to rest on his haunches by the open door, Zac held the youngster's shoulders and looked into his eyes. "Skip, you stay here in the office. I've got unfinished business across the street."

Still stooping, he looked back to the agent behind the tall counter. "His pa was killed on the coach and his mother died some years back. The company will need to look for any survivin' relatives; till then, he's with me."

The boy reached out to grab Zac's sleeve and knotted the white cloth in his little fist. "P-P-P-lease, Mr. Cobb. Don't . . . don't go." His eyes were wet with tears that by sheer will he refused to let drop.

"Son, when I was a little shaver like you, my ma would remind us children that God put parents on the earth to nudge us up to the idea that He was up there lookin' after us. They were s'posed to be His hands, His arms, and His eyes down here. 'Course they weren't really, just a remembrance. Now your ma and pa aren't here anymore, but just 'cause the remembrance is gone, don't make the fact not so. He's just as much up there lookin' after you as He always was. You just have to believe that, boy. Don't let the way things appear rule your life. Ofttimes, the things we can't see are more powerful than the things we can."

Zac stood up and gripped the brass doorknob. "Part of what a man does, Skip, is stand for what he knows to be right. You got to live right so that when the time comes to die, all you got left to do is die. Your pa did that, I believe. I got to do that too."

He took Skip's hand and, freeing the boy's fingers from his shirt, put his hand on the boy's head. "Now, you just set here and wait. I'm gonna make sure the men who did what they did to your pa and the people on that coach pay for it."

CHAPTER 12

Zachary took the watch out of his vest pocket. He sprung it open and studied the Roman numerals emblazoned on the pearl-colored face. Over an hour had passed since leaving the marshal's office. Closing it with a snap, he slipped the chain through his fingers, gently fondling the locket attached to one of its gold loops. How Jenny had come by it worried him. It wasn't tidy. The loose ends left behind in San Luis seemed to silently lie in a pool at the back of his mind, not moving, not draining, just smelling with each passing day. It wasn't like him to be distracted, but now he had a boy with no family and the locket of a woman he loved, taken off a corpse he himself had dispatched. It made him all the more anxious to get this over with and get on back home.

Opening the heart-shaped locket, he mentally drifted over the picture of Jenny. He almost wondered out loud how many times her Henry had stared at that same picture, thinking about how he too wanted to hold her, hear her voice, and kiss her lips, only to have his hopes lost at sea. Zac couldn't think about that now. He had to harden his heart and sharpen his mind. All he could allow himself to think about were the killers in the saloon across the street.

The longer he watched the front door of the Busted Flush the more impatient he became. The street was busy with miners looking for lunch, and a few women fussing over the wares of a vendor. The horses were still there, though, hard-ridden and stiff-legged. Their hindquarters were coated with a day's lather dried into salty horse hair by the desert sun. Zac uprooted his .45 and placed a sixth load under the hammer.

He scooted the holster to the left and tied the weapon to his thigh, ready for a cross draw. Withdrawing his belly gun from the shoulder holster under his vest, Zac checked the half loads and spun the cylinder, gauging the action of the puny but effective short gun. Turning to the window of the Wells Fargo office, he caught the anxious face of little Skip. The boy had the look of a man with all his chips in the middle of the table watching the last card drop. Whatever happened, Zac knew he had to come back.

He could wait no longer. He wasn't known to the holdup men inside; he'd seen them, but they'd not seen him. He was sure he could recognize them even in the dim, filtered light of a bar. Given the fact that their stakeout man hadn't caught up to them, and the banker who was the mainspring of the operation was now missing, he was sure he could recognize them by their long faces, if nothing else.

The fact that the banker had stopped to pick up the loot put those hardcases in an even more itchy state of mind. They'd be down in the mouth and madder than bobcats with their tails on fire. They'd also be plenty nervous. News of the massacre on the coach had the entire town buzzing and ready to string up anybody who was even suspected of the crime. The body Zac had brought in might have already been recognized by some passersby, and he just couldn't afford to wait any longer and allow those men to escape. He had to end this business here. Maybe arresting them would be a mercy. Zac figured to just take a corner table and keep an eye peeled till the marshal arrived. He'd have to think of a way of identifying them for sure, but till he did, he'd just keep a close watch.

As he walked across the street and patted the rump of a mustang hitched outside the saloon, something caught him up short. He thought he recognized another set of horses tied up nearby, but he put it out of his mind. Besides, he couldn't be sure.

Walking through the batwing doors and taking a seat nearest the window on the street, he tipped his hat back off his head, allowing it to dangle suspended behind his neck. The knotted rawhide chin strap tightly cut a line across his Adam's apple. Squinting his eyes, he began to survey the room. There they were. Two of the burly bandits stood at the bar. They drank beer and were sloshing down hard-boiled eggs between gulps.

The larger of the two seemed to be using a whetstone to sharpen a knife, occasionally holding it up to the light to examine its edge. Trail dust coated them from head to foot. To their left and farther back into the darkened saloon, the remaining three played a game of billiards. They surrounded the felt-covered table, and one of them straddled a massive, carved table leg, preparing to take his shot. The other two stood to the rear in the shadow of the table's overhead lamps and focused their gaze on the green surface. Zac noticed their pistols were hung on a pegboard on the back wall, and smoke curled around the dim light as the one bending over sent the balls crashing. From the other rear table farther back into the darkness he heard a familiar voice, "Damnation . . ."

Zac had contentedly accounted for all of the men he had been looking for, yet failed to notice the other dimly lit game in the very back of the room. What he couldn't place with the horses tied up out front came washing into his mind with the raspy curse that rang out from the other table. It was the McKenneys!

"Barkeep! Bring us some more whisky back here. Don't make me come and get it."

There was no place for Zac to hide and little time left before his luck would run out and the bad pennies that seemed to keep dogging his trail would show up once again and rip away his secrecy. But until he could plan his next move, the best thing to do was sit still and do nothing.

"What's the matter, barkeep, you deef or somethin'? We is thirsty back here." The mouth of old man McKenney sent shivers up Zac's spine, but hardly a head turned at the bar, so he scooted back his chair and decided to act.

He walked from his table to the front of the bar with his empty beer glass. "Beer," he said. Trying to prevent what would more than likely turn out to be a bloody and dangerous scene he added, "But before you pour mine, I think you'd better take some whisky back to those boys back there." He thought if he could subtly affect the service, it might keep the McKenneys out of eye shot and allow him to wait a little longer for the marshal.

The rotund bartender with gray muttonchops around his protruding cheeks poured Zac's beer. "I'll take care of them directly," he said. Then leaning to the side he shouted to the darkened rear table, "Keep a plug in your mouth back there, I'm working fast as a body can."

Zac slipped the watch out of his vest pocket and opened the disk to check the time. As he did, the smaller of the black-bearded bandits standing to his left caught sight of the watch and the locket that dangled from its chain. He nudged the elbow of the stocky desperado to his left, and when Zac lifted his eyes up from reading the dial, he could see their eyes harden in his direction. Something told him time had run out.

The huge bear-like bandit laid his knife on the bar and stuck the whetstone deep into his pants pocket. He stared into Zac's eyes and slowly turned to face him. The short, stumpy companion who had drawn his attention to the agent began to back away and edge himself back toward the crowded pool table, where the rest of the gang were still preoccupied with their billiards.

Zac knew that his moment of reckoning was at hand and whatever happened now would have to happen without the marshal and his promised posse. He spoke up to try to delay any immediate action.

"What's your problem? Do I know you? Look like you seen a ghost."

The man in the black beard seemed to snarl an answer, his eyes squinting, "I ain't seen no ghost. Just someone 'bout to become one!"

With that, he swept the polished blade from the top of the bar and sailed it into the air in Zac's direction. The tip of the knife landed with a "thud" and lanced into Zac's left shirt sleeve, pinning his limb to the top of the mahogany surface. While the short, stubby thief reached for his sidearm to Zac's left, the bearded knife-thrower cocked an elbow and began to pull out a heavy Colt that hung strapped to his side.

Zac made no movement to wrench his arm from the bar. Sweeping his free right hand under his vest, he plucked the belly gun from its shoulder harness. Laying the revolver across his suspended left arm, he fired two quick snap shots at the stubby bandit, who took both slugs in the belly and dropped to his knees. Wheeling around his fixed wrist, he sent three more slugs into the massive highwayman who had raised his Colt.

The huge brigand lumbered forward, unable or unwilling to fall. He placed both hands around Zac's neck while the agent wrested the knife from its anchorage and rammed it into the body of the man who seemed to envelope him. Zac firmly planted it below the rib cage and tore into the flesh with a jerking motion. The life seemed to suddenly drain from the big man. His beard raked down Zac's shirt as he crumpled to the floor.

A roar belched out from the rear of the room and a slug crashed into Zac's hip, splitting his holster and glancing off the Colt he still carried. Without stopping to look, Zac left his feet and rolled off the top of the bar, landing heavily on the catwalk that snaked behind the heavy wooden facade. Falling on his back, he rolled over and clung to the wooden slats like a lizard on an unfamiliar rock.

His Colt had spilled to the floor and the short barrel he still held in his hand was now short on shells. Scooting on his rear and putting his back to the wall, he swung his head from side to side, hoping to make whatever he had still count.

The sulfuric smell of gunpowder hung in the air like rancid pollen. Its cloud fell onto the glassware. Every muscle in Zac's body clinched, and the palm of his right hand began to sweat profusely as it clutched a meager offering in view of the three men who remained on the other side of the bar. He heard the scuffle of feet in the rear of the room and tried to lie still, hoping it was the sound of the marshal, or at least the disappearance of his foes. Cocking his head to the right, he noticed a hat slowly ascend over the end of the bar. He pointed the short gun and waited.

A pair of bushy eyebrows soon gave way to a clinched set of teeth and a surprised expression. It was Jock McKenney. The old man slowly raised his large revolver and pointed it in Zac's direction. A bright flame spouted out the long barrel and seemed to sear the sweat that was now forming a pool on the back of Zac's neck. The sound of a painful cry behind him jerked Zac around in time to see another bandit fall, the man's cocked sidearm tumbling to the floor. Turning around, he watched McKenney's teeth break into a wide, polished smile. "Come on out, boy, them other two done skedaddled."

As Zac stepped over his newly fallen foe and into the light, the marshal eased his way through the front of the saloon with gun drawn. "Tarnation, Cobb. What did you go and do to my town?"

With that remark, the back door sprung open and the two leftover stage robbers filed ahead of the McKenney boys, who had cocked weapons pressed against the unfortunate men's backbones. "Looky here, Pa, what we found us. Goin' in a hurry they was too."

The elder McKenney grinned. "Well, sir, looks like we got us some reward money a comin'. I do believe me and the boys are gonna give up that fool gold pannin' of ours and jes' foller you around, Cobb. We durn sure ain't gonna die from boredom, and along side of that, we'll be power-ful rich."

Stooping to pick up his spilt Colt, Zac saw the bear of a man he had poured half of his ammunition and a rather long knife into begin to stir. A low moan and heavy breath came out of the man's matted beard as the agent turned him over. He looked up at Zac. "You," he croaked. "You're the one."

Zac watched the man's eyes flutter as he held him up in his arms. "How? How'd you know it was me?"

The stench of beer and the smell of death came out with the dying man's last words. "The locket. We was told to look for a man with a gold heart-shaped locket." The man's eyes turned up into his eye sockets and then he collapsed, sprawled on the floor.

CHAPTER 13

Jenny wiped her brow with the back of her hand. The days had been long since she'd been without Me Che, and with the increasing tension she found herself even snapping at George. He'd cooked his last meals, cleaned the kitchen, and gone home some time ago. The lights had been turned off at the general store across the street, things were quiet, and now she was sweeping up and setting the tables for the morning breakfast crowd. From behind her back, she heard the sound of the bell on the top of the door. Still sweeping, she spoke with irritation, "Didn't you see the sign? We're closed."

Turning around, armed with broom and dustpan, she found herself facing Captain Mike Hogan. "Sorry to startle you, Jenny. I merely assumed you would want someone to look in on you. Come to think of it, I could also use a cold piece of that apple pie and some coffee, if you've got it."

"You are a fortunate man indeed, Michael Hogan. I have a pot over the coals and there is pie left. It's past my closing time, but I've got no place to go. Besides, I try never to turn down a paying customer. You are a paying customer, aren't you?"

"That I am, lass. You see a very prosperous man before you, prosperity I'd like to share with you."

"Just the part of your prosperity that pays for the pie and coffee will be fine. Set yourself down and I'll fetch you a piece."

Without sitting down, the seaman followed Jenny into the darkened kitchen and watched as she cut the pie. "I am concerned for your safety, Jenny."

She was startled at hearing his voice. She didn't realize he had followed her. "Why should you be, Michael? I'm perfectly safe here. The sheriff is down the street, and the most danger I'm in is cutting myself while peeling apples."

The captain spoke in a low tone. "You have much more to be afraid of than you know, my dear. My advice to you is to leave the matter of your waitress alone. She simply has me confused with someone else."

Jenny pushed past him with the pie and coffee-pot and placed them on the table in front of the window. Straightening her apron and dress, she answered, "Well, don't you think I know that? She is a frightened stranger in a strange place. I know just how she feels. She just stares at the ceiling in her cell, not saying much. Maybe she is confused. She does talk about her brother and the fact that she thinks you killed him, though."

"That's nonsense! And your listening to her is part of the problem. I've heard people talk," Hogan continued. "They feel you're a little too thick with the Chinese to suit their taste."

"The only part of people's taste I'm at all interested in is their mouths," Jenny shot back.

As Hogan began to put his fork into the pie, he maintained careful eye contact with Jenny, seeming to read her mind and watch the meaning of the emotions she displayed.

"Jenny, I know these people from my time in China. They are a secretive lot with great intrigue. I have heard that Me Che's brother has indeed disappeared, but because of a blood feud between families. Not at my hands!" He paused and leaned forward. "If this is indeed a feud, you could be putting yourself in mortal danger by seeming to take sides."

Jenny pulled up a chair as the captain turned to gaze out the window. He seemed to be looking for someone. Turning back to her, he spoke softly, "My fear is, Jenny, that the further you meddle in this, the more you will expose yourself to great danger from this woman's enemies. This may be California to you, but these people live in a different world. Their underground China is more commanding than any sheriff and most assuredly of greater magnitude than any soldier-agent from a stagecoach company."

The warning from Hogan did little to unsettle Jenny's thoughts, but the fact that he knew of Zac's other job did disturb her. *No one knows about that!* she thought. Clearing her throat, she spoke up, "What do I know about stage lines or their agents? I just serve food to their customers."

The captain made no response. He just put another bite of pie into his mouth and sipped his strong coffee. "The locket I returned to you must tell you something about the trouble I would go to for your benefit. I feel something of a responsibility to you for the sake of an old friend."

Jenny bit her lip, hoping he wouldn't ask her what had happened to the necklace. "Do you have it with you?" he asked.

Trying to avoid the issue, she responded, "I've been wondering, Michael, given the fact that the *Blue Swan* was lost at sea, how did you come by Henry's locket?"

Sipping his coffee, he thought through his answer. "He maintained a house in Hong Kong, Jenny. Most sailors have little desire to sleep aboard ship when they put into port. The locket was stored in a box on his desk."

Wiping the perspiration from her hands on her apron she said, "I wouldn't have thought he'd let it out of his sight. I'd never known him to take it off of his neck."

The captain studied her over the top of the cup. "If it had been me, Jenny, I would never have taken it off. In fact, I had a hard time giving it back to you. I'd become quite attached to it. Just opening it up from time to time and seeing your picture drew me closer to Henry and to you, even though I'd never met you. Lonely sailors do have their attachments." He reached across the table and placed his hand on top of hers, patting it softly. "Do you have it with you?"

There was no longer any way to avoid the pain of telling the truth, and no matter how much it hurt, he would have to find out sooner or later. She pulled her hand out from under his. "I'm sorry, Michael, I slipped it into Zac's pocket when he left town last week."

The blow to the captain's pride could be seen through the steam of his coffee, but Jenny quickly continued to explain, hoping to soften the shock. "Zachary Cobb has been a good friend these years here in San Luis. In fact, he even loaned me the money to get set up in this place." She was feeling increasingly defensive and nervous, and it made her angry.

"Is this a serious thing?" he asked. "This friendship with Mr. Cobb."

Jenny pushed herself slightly back from the table. "Captain, I don't know who taught you manners, but ladies do not like to discuss their feelings in such matters. But even though it's none of your business, I will tell you this: I don't believe Mr. Cobb is serious about anything but his work and that seaside ranch he owns."

Reaching across the table, the captain took her hand again. "Jenny, if you will allow me to express my feelings for you at some appropriate time, I am sure you will find them to be much plainer and quite sincere. My only desire is for your security and happiness."

Instinctively, she pulled away and busied herself with clearing his dishes. He reached out again and took her wrist. Looking into her startled eyes, he said, "Right now, I must admit, Jenny, my greatest concern is for your *safety*. I fear you are up against forces of which you have no idea, ones that could destroy you in a heartbeat."

"Michael, I'm afraid I'll have to go about my business and protect myself the best way I know how. I do appreciate your concern, in any event. By the way, how is your shoulder?"

Reaching up to massage his right upper arm he said, "It's stiff and pains me greatly. Considering the target your girl had in mind, however, I find myself quite lucky."

She knew she shouldn't have said it even as it was coming out of her mouth, but she was a little frightened by how the man had been making her feel and felt like striking back at him in the only place he seemed to be vulnerable, his ego. "Well, as you can see, Captain, you have your hands full with defending yourself, let alone trying to protect me."

What she said seemed to have the desired effect. The man sat stone still and blinked as if he had been hit between the eyes with a brick. She scrambled to her feet and left him sitting there alone while she returned the dishes to the kitchen. He was still sitting at the table staring out the window when she returned.

After blowing out the lights and closing the doors, Jenny said good-night to the captain and began the short walk down the street to check on Me Che. In the darkness, a match was struck to light a cigarette. The figure who held it kept pace with her steps, pausing to avoid passing a well-lit saloon window. Jenny quickened her walk and turned the knob on the door to the sheriff's office.

Closing the door behind her, she noticed the deputy with his feet on the desk. "Hello, Fred, is Jeff in the office?" she asked.

"No, ma'am, he isn't, and I'd like to get some word to him if you see him. He's out chasing shadows on this Chinese lady's problems, and it ain't needed."

"What do you mean it isn't needed? She has rights too."

Fred rose from the desk and shrugged his shoulders. "I 'spose yer right, Miss Jenny. Though I don't generally think of Chinese people and rights as two things that go together. Fact is, though, ma'am, she ain't here no more."

Jenny was startled. "I don't understand. Where is she?"

"Well, a couple of hours ago, this here Captain Hogan came in and dropped all the charges. Durned if that didn't beat all. Didn't think it was such a good idea to let her out myself, what with the sheriff being gone and all, but he insisted. I tried to tell him she just might try to kill him again if we didn't cipher this out, but he said he'd be in no danger. How do you figure that?"

"I don't know, Fred, but I don't like it either. I just saw Michael Hogan not more than ten minutes ago, and he never mentioned doing that. I don't like it at all."

"Yes, ma'am."

"Where did Jeff go?"

"The sheriff said he was a going down to the railhead to find out if they knew anything about this here woman's brother. Most of these young Chinamen work for the railroad, you know. Guess he just thought they might have some kinda word on the fella's whereabouts."

Jenny stood there, thinking out loud to the deputy. "It just doesn't make sense. That captain doesn't have an ounce of compassion for the Chinese. Why should he just release her? And why would he be at my place just now eating pie and not say anything? Can you understand it?"

"No, ma'am."

"Unless, of course, there was money in it for him somewhere." She stood, thinking. "This will stop the sheriff's investigation, no doubt."

"Yes, ma'am."

Jenny turned to leave and said, "When Jeff gets back, tell him I went home and ask him to drop in on me before he heads back to his place."

"Yes, ma'am, I surely will do that. He said he'd be back here before he went home, and his wife's already been here asking after him. Got a cold supper and a cold shoulder waiting on him when he does get back. He surely does now. If you'll wait a few minutes, ma'am, I'm heading up your way on patrol. Be glad to see you home."

"Thank you, Fred, but I'll be all right. I've had enough offers of protection for one night. It's been a long day and I'm in a hurry to get back."

Jenny pulled the shawl tightly around her

shoulders as she began the march back to the cafe. Her small but cozy apartment occupied the second story above the dining room. She walked quickly but quietly. The anxiety of her evening had forged a longing for a good book and a cup of tea to drive away the questions and fears in her mind.

Passing the darkened storefronts across from the blazing lights and blaring music of the El Sombrero Saloon, her eyes explored the gloom and her ears strained, trying to catch any sound of the stranger who had kept pace with her minutes before. She stepped off the boardwalk, not looking to her left down the dark alley, and not seeing the glow of a cigarette and the patch of red beard it illuminated.

CHAPTER 14

Bridger's head felt like the weight of a freight wagon was pressing it into the floor. His eyes were still closed and there wasn't an ounce of energy or effort he wanted to expend in trying to open them. From the tips of his fingers, he could sense a texture that felt like carpet. It puzzled his buzzing brain and he stayed the longest time down on his belly trying to figure out how carpet could have gotten under him and what the noise was he was hearing on the other side of the room.

Against his better judgment and with a feeling of pain, he pulled open his eyelids. They seemed sticky, as if sealed by a hardened glue. One by one his eyelashes jerked open, allowing soft yellow lantern light to filter into his foggy brain.

He lay like a large lump on the carpet while two strong arms reached over him, turning him onto his back. His head hurt like blazes with every movement of his body, and when he was finally turned, he stared up at an indistinct figure. The darkly clothed man stood over him, while his own body seemed to be swirling about in a whirlpool of disorientation. The sheriff's eyes blinked and his world took shape enough to vaguely make out the figure standing over him. It was the young

Chinese swordsman he had thrown out the window several days before.

The young man backed away and Bridger turned his head, surveying the room. Lanterns hung from the ceiling, each cased in a square parchment that softened the light to a quiet glow. The furniture was red and black, and at the far end of the room sat an elderly man with white hair. He sat with the toes of his gold slippers pointing at the big, helpless man on the floor, and he slowly drew tobacco smoke through a white, long-stemmed clay pipe.

Responding to a subtle motion of one of the old man's hands, four strong young men gingerly lifted Bridger from the floor and placed him onto a group of pillows facing the old man. As they moved away, a young girl with a red silk gown came forward and wiped his forehead and eyes with a warm, wet cloth. She pressed a small teacup filled with warm liquid into his hand and, bowing slowly, disappeared toward the rear of the room.

Bridger blinked and looked at the old man, focusing first on his rich robes and long white mustache and then more intently on his eyes. Cataracts had slowly eclipsed the old man's sight. The elderly man's eyes slowly blinked, forming a glaze over milky white clouds that had covered each pupil. The white disks looked like two cloudy moons hung on a summer's night. They hid the old man from viewing people, but his mind seemed sharp as he listened to the Chinese words from his strongmen. Staring at each person in turn while they spoke to him, he seemed to float through their words like a ghost in a grave-yard.

He fixed his empty eyes on Bridger, lightly inhaling his pipe, and spoke. "Welcome to my humble home, honorable Sheriff. Please drink your tea. It very special ginseng herbal tea. It will steady your head."

Bridger raised his hand to touch the bandages wound around his throbbing skull, bandages he couldn't remember being applied. "Much obliged," he replied. "If it will help my head, I'll need a lot more of it." He tried to force a painful grin. "I'm also grateful to whoever went to the trouble of this."

He pointed to the gauze wrapped around his head. Realizing his host couldn't see his gesture, he spoke apologetically, "I was speaking about the wrappings on my head."

The old man smiled. "You need not apologize, Mr. Bridger. I have no need to see you with my outer eyes to understand you. I see no more with these eyes." The old gentleman raised a finger, gesturing to his chalk-white pupils. "I have seen you often with my soul."

Bridger's brows arched and a puzzled look quietly erupted on his face.

The old man continued, "I see with my ears and through the eyes of my children."

The old man spread his hands apart and pointed toward each side of the room, where young Chinese men and women quietly bowed to his gesture.

"I see you when you walk through my streets and ask about two young people I am sworn to protect. I see you with my ears when you broke my shop door. I see you when you instructed my young highbinders on how a man is to use his body. And I see you on the road when the men dropped what they thought was your dead body. You would have died too, had it not been for my young men here and the kindness of my grand-daughters."

He lifted his index finger in the sheriff's direction, and the girl quickly refilled Bridger's cup with more of the steaming brew. "When my children see, I see. They see. They tell everything. I quietly think on what I learn and give instructions. I teach. They are learning to be better students, but we have much yet to do." He swung his head from side to side, and the young men who flanked him seemed penitently to bow their heads and lower their eyes.

"These my children have much yet to learn and I am still here to teach them until I die."

"I can't recall ever seeing you in town, Mr. . . . I'm afraid you have me at an unfair advantage. You know who I am, but I don't know you."

Drawing his lips tightly around the thin stem of the pipe, the old man waved the escaping smoke back into his face. "I am Hong Lee, Grand Master of the Kwong Dock Tong. I care for welfare of my children, provide them harmless diversions,

164

and allow businesses to flourish. I bring about wisdom and justice for my people. You see, you and I are in the same position in this village."

Bridger smiled and replied, "I do my darndest to take care of the justice around here, but rarely get into the wisdom business."

"Then allow me, Mr. Bridger, to give you the rewards of my wisdom. I do know you to be a man of justice. I hear much. You must know of what I hear. You have powerful enemies. They have already attempted to kill you. The next time they will not speculate on your death and drop you on the road. These are my enemies as well. They smuggle in new Chinese people all the time, people who are not part of the Kwong Dock. My people have a saying in their land, 'The enemy of my enemy is my friend.' We are very different, Mr. Bridger, but today you and I are friends."

Bridger's eyes roamed around the richly decorated room. Brightly colored cloth that formed the robes of the old wise man was woven with what appeared to be gold and silver threads, and in the corner of the room an incense burner of pure gold sifted the bold odor of jasmine into the air. "We are very different, Mr. Lee." The sheriff sipped his tea and smelled the rich aroma before adding, "You know it's been my experience that friendship means trust. It would be mighty hard for you to trust someone like me."

The old man's mustache curled up with a subtle smile. "You are a wise man, Mr. Bridger. I sense what you mean is that you yourself would find it hard to trust the Kwong Dock. You say your mind not to offend. This is good. We understand each other more than you know. Let us speak to each other like men, not as children playing."

Bridger nodded. Catching his nonverbal message, he grunted, "Go ahead."

"The men of the railroad desire the labor of my people, but repay them with injustice. They supply the old fathers and the younger empty-headed ones with opium instead of honest wages. I spent many years in Hong Kong dealing with the British."

"That must be where you learned your good English."

"You are quite right, Mr. Bridger. And in dealing with the British, I found a people who wanted to sell the opium to my people to gain power. To the weak-minded, the white powder is power. This is a power that we of the Tong have exercised with justice through the years. Now, the wide-eyed men of your railroad want to take that away from us. We cannot give the power of our souls over to the people of your world. These builders of the iron dragon keep my people as slaves instead of men. They abuse the women for their own pleasure and threaten to burn their humble homes if they complain. These men and the murderous lackey sailors who serve them are a darkness to my soul. They are trying to put out the light in my children's minds."

The big sheriff's head throbbed, and he was

growing more impatient for the man to come to the point. He leaned forward and placed his now empty teacup on the black lacquered table beside him. "How can I help you and your people, Mr. Lee?"

"We live in two worlds together," the old man continued. "We cannot approach your world for justice. We cannot directly oppose our enemies who are round eyes. What we must do is allow others to do this for us. The soulless businessmen from the Iron Dragon have brought their own white powder to these shores through their own ships. They tried to steal our own shipment, but a brave yet ignorant farmer, who unknowingly was transporting it, prevented them. This shipment has since disappeared."

Bridger's mind immediately flashed back to the men who had attempted to rob Zachary Cobb. What had seemed like a simple robbery by sailors now took on greater weight. The puzzle piece represented by the bags of the powder being shipped in barrels of whale oil also made a clean fit.

"I believe I found your missing shipment, Mr. Lee. Found it right before my lights went out." Jeff put his hand up to his throbbing temple, trying to arrest the pain with a little outside pressure.

"It might help with explaining the disappearance of Miss Che's brother if you could tell me if he knew where you stored the shipment after it arrived."

The old man smiled and nodded. "The young man not only knew but was trusted with its safe-keeping. When the opium disappeared so did the young man. There is much talk about this powder. But it is not against your law, nor is it the issue at hand."

"No, Mr. Lee. Opium can be bought in any drugstore. But the smuggling of your people has been stopped. If that's going on in my district, I'm bound to put a stop to it. What I can't figure out is why you would care who's bringing the opium in."

"It is power, Mr. Bridger. That is the issue at hand. The white powder is power. I use it mercifully for the benefit of my children. The men of the iron dragon use it to make them simple slaves. Whoever supplies it has the power. My people who smoke it will do anything for it, and I must see that it is given to them by my own benevolent hands and not by the claws of men of the iron dragon." The old man paused as if holding a trump card that would get the attention of the big lawman.

"The young Chinese man you seek; he was an informer for the Kwong Dock. It is he who discovered how the men of the iron dragon were bringing in more opium. He made contact with them; now he is dead or missing." He paused to puff on his clay pipe. "Of course," he said, "no one can arrest the murderer of one of our people in this country."

Bridger didn't bother to disagree with the old

man. He knew what the sage said was indeed true. "Let me put it this way for you, Mr. Lee; I'll do my best to serve justice for everybody in this county, you can count on that."

"The young businesswoman of the eating establishment . . ." The old man paused to let the effect of what he was going to say drive deep into the sheriff's thinking. "She is also a prisoner of these same men. Find the opium, and you will find the woman. You will also find the kidnappers of Me Low."

"Something's happened to Jenny?"

The old man sat silently and nodded his head.

"I've got to go find her." He shook his head. "You were in Hong Kong, did you know an American sea captain there named Henry Taylor?"

"Yes, Mr. Bridger, I knew him."

"Well, the woman you speak of was engaged to marry him, before his ship went down."

The old man sat and silently thought over what Bridger had said. "I not know where you heard this, Mr. Bridger, but Mr. Taylor's ship did not go down. He was murdered and his ship is being used now to bring slaves to this country for the iron dragon."

The old gentleman rose to his feet and steadied himself on the arms of the two muscular young men who stood on either side of him. "It is late for me. I have my cart at the door. You do me the honor of having it take you to rest in your own home. One last warning; beware of the one who comes to you to help you. Beware of the stranger with a smile." With that the old man's face seemed to crease into a subtle grin. He turned and was led away to his rest.

The ride on the donkey cart was slow and labored, and the young men who rode with the sheriff said little during the long ride to the Bridger ranch. The immaculate interior of the cart was lined with polished wood that was shined with great regularity. His escorts on the trip were three young pigtailed highbinders, each sporting an iron hand axe tucked into his belt. To his side rode the young man he had thrown down the stairs.

"Sorry about what happened the other day," Bridger said. "I hope you weren't cut by the glass." The young man merely sat in uncomfortable silence, never returning Bridger's overtures or taking his eyes off the direction they were heading. The cart pulled into the front of the sheriff's house, and the young man spun his head around to speak.

"You are home to your wife tonight because the Grand Master wishes it so. We expect no help from you, no favors. We expect only more breaking down our doors and more white justice. But you . . . you need not worry. I must oversee after your safety. It is wish of the Grand Master and I am his *boo how doy*."

Bridger watched as the wheels of the cart spun down the road back to town and studied the hanging lanterns while they bounced about the rear of the carriage roof. He hoped some poor drunk cowboy didn't decide to stop the funny cart and yahoo these Chinamen on their way home.

Evangeline put him right to bed after he had looked in on the sleeping children. It gave him great peace to know that somewhere in the world of hate and suspicion he was mired in, there were still children that slept, his children. Evangeline tucked him in and he decided not to explain his night on the job just yet. Her hair was down and brushed. She had wound its beautiful brown texture into braids, which was her custom at night, and in no time had appeared at his bedside with a steaming broth to take the chill out of his body.

"I was so worried," she said. "When Jenny's friend, that nice Captain Hogan, brought back the sorrel, he said he was going back to look for you. We both thought that blame thing had thrown you and kicked your head in."

CHAPTER 15

Jenny blinked, trying to accustom her eyes to the dim light that filtered into her confined space. She felt woozy and her head throbbed with each beat of her heart. The movement she sensed beneath her, a swaying motion she was unaccustomed to feeling, added to her discomfort. Lifting her head, she tried to focus her eyes on the shaft of light that filtered through a small, odd-shaped window.

I must be on board a ship, she thought. *How did I ever get here?*

She struggled to lift herself up from the swaying cot, but the pain that still pulsated through her head made sitting up too difficult, and she collapsed on the bunk with a groan. She heard the bolt slide on the outside of the door and decided to lie still and pretend to be out of commission. Shutting her eyes as the door opened and closed, she heard the scuffling of bare feet, then the sound of water poured into a basin. A chapped hand stroked her forehead and a wet cloth was applied to the top of her scalp. She steadied her breathing, trying hard not to gasp.

A whispered rasp spoke her name. "Miss Jenny. Miss Jenny. I hope you not hurt bad, Miss Jenny."

Tiataglo! Her eyes bolted open and just as

quickly the weathered harpooner put his hand over her mouth. "Please, Miss Jenny. No speak, please. If Captain ketch me here wif you, ma'am, I be in great difficulty. I take my hand off you now, but please speak soft." She nodded her head as he lifted his large hand.

Her lips trembled as she whispered, "Tiataglo, what am I doing here? How did I get to this place?"

"Miss Jenny, I not know for sure. Big Irish Mick, the first mate, he bring you on board last night. He evil man, Missy, but I think he only follow orders. Captain Hogan put you in here and lock the door. You okay?"

"My head is swimming in pain, but I believe I am all right." She started to sit up. "I've got to get out of here, Tiataglo. I've got to go home."

The powerful man held her shoulders. "You can't go now, Miss Jenny. Too many sailor mans topside. They bring on fresh water. Captain says we sail tomorrow night with the tide."

"Sail! I can't go! Where is he taking me?"

"He say we go to San Francisco. He say he want to take you to a doctor there. But we taking on too many supplies and too much water for San Francisco. I think we go Shanghai."

"China! I can't go to China!"

"Please, Miss Jenny, you talk too loud."

She struggled to get up. "Tiataglo, you've got to help me get off this ship."

"I hep you, Miss Jenny, but I no can do now. You gonna haf to wait."

As the seaman started to speak, they were both alarmed by the sound of the hatch sliding above the stairway that led to the catwalk outside their cabin. Heavy-soled steps descending the stairs and the clang of a sheathed sword bouncing down the polished steps told them their uninvited third party could be no one else but Mike Hogan.

Tiataglo sprang to his feet and with a panicked look scoured the room. With several leaps, he rushed to the curtained nook in the corner of the room that served as a storage compartment.

Jenny pressed herself into the bedding and stilled her breathing. Her eyelids closed in clenched darkness as the sound of footsteps paused outside her cabin. *He can see the door is unlocked,* she thought.

Quietly, it opened and she could sense the captain standing above her prone body, standing and watching her measured breathing. She wanted to simply lie there and hope he would disappear from where he came, but as her mind raced she knew that to prolong the inevitable meeting one moment more might mean he would search the cabin, might mean he would find Tiataglo, might mean disaster.

She opened her eyes, expecting to make eye contact; instead she saw Hogan standing over her, quietly eyeing her still form. The thought of being inspected like a piece of meat in the butcher shop made her shiver. Their eyes finally met.

"Oh, you're awake," he said.

"Yes. Why am I here? What right have you to

bring me to this place?"

He shrugged his shoulders and held his hands up in innocence. "I warned you of the dangers you were facing. If my man hadn't found you last night, the thugs that attacked you might have killed you."

"What thugs are you talking about? I saw no such thing. The last thing I remembered was someone grabbing me from behind and some foul-smelling cloth being placed over my face. I still feel it when I swallow."

"That's what I was trying to tell you about. The people who see you interfering with them are devious creatures who will stop at nothing to ruin me."

"What does that have to do with me?" she asked. "Your enemies, Captain Hogan, are yours, not mine. I want off this ship at once."

She sat up on the bed and, rolling her legs under her, scooted to the top of the bunk as the hulking sailor paced around her narrow bed. "I'm afraid that will not be possible, my dear. I know you're an innocent girl from a small town, and perhaps these matters are much too devious for you to understand, but for your own sake, and for the memory of my friend Henry, you'll have to trust me."

From the corner of her eye, Jenny watched the curtain slowly draw aside. Tiataglo was behind the captain, silently edging his way to the open door. With panic tumbling through her stomach, she picked up the pace of her conversation, trying to keep the captain's attention. "Michael Hogan, trust is something you give to someone. It isn't taken. It isn't drugged, and most certainly, it isn't locked up."

She tried hard not to look at the curtain or focus in any way on the creeping figure of the harpooner who was quietly padding his way to the open door. But when the words "locked up" escaped her breath, she knew she had made a reference she would regret. As the lanky captain began to swing his head toward the door, she shot out her hand and took hold of his collar. Drawing the bearded face toward her, the petite woman lifted her back from the soft pillows.

"I stopped allowing other people to protect me when I left my father's home. I have not signed on to your crew. I am not a child and you, dear captain, will never take my Henry's place." She spat out the words so rapidly they escaped her lips without benefit of thought. Her eyes widened and their blue tint hardened into the color of a stormy sky.

As the islander slipped silently through the door, Hogan riveted his stare into Jenny's blustery face and with great calm stated, "My dear, I know you're upset and that the drugs those brigands subjected you to last night have played havoc with your disposition, but I trust a sea voyage and a competent San Francisco doctor can settle your thinking."

"Michael Hogan, I wouldn't trust you far enough to walk around the block with you, to say nothing about a sea voyage. You release me this instant!"

The captain said nothing. He only turned and walked to the door.

Jenny followed him. The anger boiled up inside her and came out in a hushed, seething whisper. "You sea snake, the slave trade seems to be your only talent." With that, each succeeding phrase rose in intensity and volume. "You haven't chosen a timid girl from China this time. You won't get the slightest amount of cooperation from me as long as you live." She pinned her hands to her sides and clenched her fists. "You disgust me."

The captain stood at the door and coldly looked her over. He wanted to strike out at her, but instead uncoiled a final prediction. "I know you're angry now, many women are at first, when they find themselves on the *Blue Goose*, but you'll feel better after you've warmed my bed for a few months."

He whirled, and, striding out the door, slammed and locked it.

Jenny collapsed to her knees and pounded on the hard oak, sobbing inconsolably.

Life at the railhead had the appearance of normalcy, except for the laughter. The night before had been celebrated with the private stock from O'Brien's car being opened. Laughter and cigar smoke poured out from the windows of the ornate red coach. The casual worker or coolie didn't try to understand the private office celebration; they were just thankful the bosses were otherwise occupied.

Breakfast had just begun in the mess tent when a rider who had galloped straight from town rode up and drew rein outside the red private car. The horseman scarcely allowed the dust to settle when he bounded through the door. Several minutes passed before a cascade of Irish curses from the car's window was followed by the red-haired brute storming out the door and toward the telegraph shack. Still steaming, O'Brien emerged from the shack a short time later. Grim determination painted his pink face, and behind his back a telegraph key violently clattered a staccato drumbeat down the wires.

O'Brien turned to one of his foremen on the porch of the telegraph shack and, taking the smoldering cigar out of his mouth, squinted his eyes against the sun and pulled down his brown derby to cut the glare. "By God, this won't happen again. Nobody's coming into my operation and talking to me the way that big hayseed did yesterday. Make that for sure in this world and in the world to come. Ian O'Brien is not a man to be trifled with. These yellow boys won't scare me, and the lug with a star on his chest and a head that is far too hard will not talk down to me again. I had enough of those shenanigans on the docks of New York."

He turned to look directly into the face of the foreman and blew a column of black smoke out the side of his pouting lips. "The company is sending a special team of troubleshooters. They should be here by nightfall. We're all going to be about the shooting of some very big trouble." The remark brought a satisfied grin from the ruddy face of the big Irishman and a responding grin from the foreman. "These lads are professionals," he remarked. "Go fix 'em up some bunks in one of the other cars."

For Zac, the ride to the ranch was the longest ride of his life. His head was buzzing. Never before had he been forced to explain himself and the reasons behind everything he did. The curiosity of a nine-year-old was beginning to wear him out, and when they reached the shoreline of the Pacific and rode north, Zac's problem intensified. The boy had never before seen the ocean.

"What are th-th-th . . . those th-th-th . . . things?" Skip asked.

"They call them sandpipers."

"Do th-th-th . . . they f-f-f . . . fly?" The boy's difficulty in getting his words out didn't stop him from asking.

"Yes, they fly."

"Th . . . they look f-f-f . . . funny, k-k-k . . . kinda like p-p-p . . . people in the circus on t-t-t . . . tall sticks."

"Stilts, Skipper, stilts." The boy was silent and Zac looked at him. "Can you say stilts?" Zac asked.

The boy shook his head and lowered his eyes.

They rode on in silence down the beach. Finally Zac asked, "Tell me — how long have you had trouble with your speech? When did it start?"

"I t-t-t . . . told you, it was when my m-m-m . . . mother died." The boy dropped his chin and his eyes misted.

"Well, son, don't worry none about it. Everybody's got something wrong with them. Sometimes it's something you can see and hear, but most of the time it's a problem inside, where it can't be seen. Harder to deal with that, I'd say. Your problem ain't as bad as most, not near as bad as mine. The important thing is to be yourself. People will learn to take you like you are."

They rode on in silence for some time before the boy looked over at Zac. "Mr. Cobb, I t-t-t . . . take you like you are, do you t-t-t . . . take me like I am?"

"Yeah, partner. 'Course I take you like you are. I wouldn't change a thing." His own statement suddenly made Zac feel a little self-conscious and restless. "Come on, boy," he said, "let's stretch these horses out a might." With that, he touched his Spanish spurs to the sides of the big Appaloosa and stormed up the beach, followed by the little boy kicking the sides of his horse for all he was worth.

As they rounded the bend near the bay, the base of Moro Rock came into clear view and produced the unusual sight of a ship being loaded in the seldom-used harbor.

Zac brought the Appaloosa to a halt and pushed his peaked hat from the top of his head.

The strap hung across his neck and he ran both his hands through his thick black hair and then stretched his shoulders, waiting for the boy to catch up.

"Now that's a puzzlement!" he exclaimed.

"I th-th-th . . . think it's great!" The boy's eyes were wide at the sight of a clipper ship and he was beginning to express himself more freely.

"Oh, it's a great sight, all right. It's just that I'd expect a ship like that to be loaded up in Cambria. Cambria's a harbor up the coast, near the ranch. They've got a long dock up there, which comes in mighty handy for vessels this size. Moro Bay, here, is a place used mostly by fishing boats. You see, a ship that size has to sit in the harbor and bring everything out by longboat. That's a pretty cumbersome task."

Skip continued to stare at the longboats loading from the shore. Zac smiled at the boy and put his suspicions aside for the time being. "Let's get on, son, we still got a ways to go yet."

CHAPTER 16

Zac found the bed hard to get used to. Being on horseback, stagecoach, and sleeping on the ground for the last three weeks had accustomed his body to harshness and discomfort. Climbing onto the feather platform suspended on a rope-weave oak bed suddenly made him feel uneasy and restless. There was too much to do, and tired as he felt, he knew he dared not get too comfortable or sleep too soundly. After listening to the wind whistle over the chimney for a while, he got up and threw a blanket in front of the empty fireplace, then lay down on it and fell asleep.

When his eyes popped open in the morning, he lay stone still. The ceiling was already sunlit, and he quietly listened to the sounds of being home. Then he berated himself for being down while the sun was up.

"Throw de corn out der. Dem chickens is mucho hungry. Sí, and the cook, he not like us to be late for breakfast. But, we hafta finish the chores before we go in."

Francisco was evidently showing Skip the ropes before breakfast. He was a natural with children. His days off were most often spent with family and his herd of little nieces, nephews, and cousins. He brought them to the hacienda by the wagonload. Zac was sure Skip wouldn't have to worry about finding friends with Fernando showing him around.

Zac continued to lie on the sheep pelt rug and let his mind drift, wondering about Jenny, when Hans broke into his thinking. "All right, Herr Cobb! It is past time that you put your slothfulness down and get up. The bacon is done, the coffee is hot, and I have made for you and your young friend my very special apple strudel."

Hans turned abruptly on his heels and marched back through the swinging main room doors. He started to go out to the cook shack, but standing before the open outer door, he wheeled about and marched back to deliver one last order. "First you must go out and wash up, then you may get the young gentleman and Francisco."

Turning about-face, the old cook smartly went back to what was left of the breakfast business. Hans had been a cook in the Prussian army for many years. *He may not be in a war,* Zac thought, *but he's still in the Prussian army.*

Zac pulled on his jeans and crammed his feet into his boots before meandering out to the water. Plunging his head into the open bucket, he came up dripping and shook his head at the already hot sun. Then he blinked his eyes and raked his fingers through his hair.

It had been a year of very little rain, and the heat was beginning to turn everything green to gold and everything gold to brown. Zac let the well water drip from his wet hair to his back and down his glistening bare chest. The streams had long since gone dry, but he was thankful for the few springs on his property that managed to slake the thirst of much of the livestock. They even kept a few wild flowers blooming here and there.

He squinted and shaded his eyes to survey the brown hills and the oaks that dotted the scorched landscape encircling the hacienda. Through the shimmering morning sun, he spotted a lone rider. A big man, on a big horse. Zac grunted and thought, *He never quits. Has a home with a wife and kids and he's still in that saddle hours before sunup.*

"*Ach du lieber!* You get yourselves to this table right now."

Hans' voice was something like a sickle dragged across a shingled roof, but right now it sounded pretty good. Still, there was not much pleasure in settin' his feet under a table without Jenny there. Why he'd allowed himself to sleep so long still bothered Zac. Maybe the long trips were wearing him down and the comfort of his own walls was just too intoxicating. Right now, home felt like a jug of barleycorn in the head of a fifteen-year-old.

"Set one more place for breakfast, Hans," he called out. "Bridger's coming up the road. It's breakfast for us, but it'll be lunch for him," he muttered. Zac scuffed his boots on the ground and wondered if any news was riding in with the sheriff. He knew he couldn't handle another telegram or another assignment just now.

After breakfast, Zac hurriedly strapped down his saddle on the back of his favorite dun mare. After hearing Bridger's report on Jenny's absence, he wasn't sure where to start looking for her, but he couldn't forget the last time he saw her as the stage rolled away. And the memory of that sea-going freight hauler walking out of the restaurant to stand beside her made him think that wherever that man was had to be the place to start looking.

"Jeff, the first place I want to look is that clipper in Moro Bay. Has no business there, no how."

The sheriff talked to Zac while he worked on his big stud's rear hoof. "If you think that's where she might be, I'd say we'd better get on it right quick. When I went by that way, they were taking on fresh water and that's generally the last to go."

"Yeah, but the tide won't let 'em out of that narrow channel till sometime tonight." Zac, matter-of-fact like, began thumbing shells into two spare bandoleers. It was almost as if he was preparing for war, but his voice didn't betray his concern or nervousness. He'd learned to treat danger as a part of the job — and yet, this wasn't his job. This was personal. He dug his hand into the broken box and slipped the shells into the worn leather. "I do think we'd best be moving along," Zac said. "I told Francisco we'd take him with us; he's handy in a pinch."

Slinging the belts of ammo over his head and glancing up across the rump of the mare, Zac pieced together where Skip had disappeared to after breakfast. The boy was leading a little sorrel out of the horse corral, saddled and ready to go.

"Now, looky here, partner," Zac called out. "Where do you think you're going?"

"I want t-t-t . . . to go with you, Mr. Cobb."

Looking into the boy's eyes, Zac could see back through the years and recognize the fear of lonesomeness. He knew all too well what the thought of being alone on the earth could do to a person's insides.

He had gone into the war trying to do his duty and looking to discover faraway places and adventure. But when it was over, he stood beside those graves out back of his Georgia home with woodworm burrowing into his soul. The pink heart that beat softly in his chest before the war had become blood-red, banging a hard staccato funeral march. He had walked out to that road for months afterward, waiting for those three brothers to come walking home. But each time he stood and watched, all he saw was an empty road, emptiness, and loneliness.

Zac stooped down beside the boy. Pushing the black hat back from the youngster's forehead, he exposed the yellow shock of hair.

"I w-w-w . . . would feel a lot safer, w-w-w . . . with you, Mr. Cobb," the boy stammered.

"Listen here, little friend, you'll actually be much safer here with Hans. Don't let them gray hairs in his beard fool you none. He's a soldier first and a cook second. I'd a thought you could have figured that out with that foul coffee he served up this morning." Zac smiled, then pointed to an oak tree in the distance. "Old Hans could take that Spencer he lugs around and put a pattern into that oak tree you could cover up with a silver dollar. And if you think he's mean, you ain't seen nothing till you see the way he treats someone stepping in his shadow."

The nine-year-old blinked at Zac and started a protest that didn't get very far. Zac went on, "Don't let him scare you none though, Skipper. He likes you. You don't for one minute think he baked that apple concoction for Francisco and me, now do you? No, son, I can't take you. It might be dangerous for you, and it surely would be dangerous for me. I'd spend so much time looking around for where you were, I might forget to duck, myself."

"Hey, little amigo." Francisco motioned his hand to Skip. "I have something for you. I have this top I carve for you this morning. It still need to be painted. I think I paint it red, with gold around the edges. What you think, little amigo? You like it, yes?"

The boy nodded. Francisco took out a string and wound it around the top, slinging it on the smooth surface of the flagstones that surrounded the large well. It clicked and skipped across the stones and momentarily diverted the boy's attention. Zac turned his back on the boy and began checking his supply of ammunition while Skip meandered away to answer the summons of his new friend, Francisco.

Bridger stared at Zac from across the back of his horse. It was a quizzical look. "You're a plumb puzzlement, Cobb. Don't believe I heard you say more words in the last five years than you said this morning at breakfast to that kid. You don't suppose you're turning into a family man now, do you?"

Zac took out his pipe, packed it with Virginia tobacco, and popped a flame on the end of his match. He lit the bowl and gazed into the hot sun. "That blasted sun, and no rain clouds. If we don't get some soon, I'll start losing cattle."

"Cobb," Bridger shot back. "Answer my question."

"What question?"

"You seem like you're in a different world, Cobb. I know you're worried about Jenny, even if you won't admit it, but I'm wondering if looking after the kid is getting to you."

"Yeah, it troubles me. Since Skip's been with me, I feel like I got to explain everything; where I'm going and why, when I'll be back, why I do every little thing I'm doing. I also started talking to him to make sure he's holding steady in his own mind. It's made me madder than hops. Still, Skip's just a child and he depends on me. Guess it just makes him feel more included to know what's going on in my head."

Bridger smiled. "Maybe you got room in that cold heart of yours for one or two more."

Zac continued to puff on his pipe and tighten his cinch. He knew he didn't want to answer that remark. He was well aware of the changes in his life that the boy had made. He had even changed the way he spoke. He no longer snapped off gruff and threatening commands. He was speaking softer, he was apologizing from time to time, and to make matters worse, he heard himself making constant chatter about what he planned to do and why.

Icy silence had been a characteristic of his past. He would brood about things that he should have talked about. Jenny had often complained to him about his annoying habit of sealing his thoughts up inside his head. Now little Skip had him purposefully explaining his actions, instead of doing silently what he knew was best and just allowing people to guess at his reasoning.

Zac turned to Bridger and repeated his new-found habit of thinking out loud, "I feel responsible for that boy and I know how he feels."

The big sheriff turned and just looked Zac in the eye.

"I do," Zac went on to explain. "This may sound very strange to you, Jeff, but in some way that boy and Jenny are connected. Whoever sent orders to the banker that the kid did away with told that whole bunch to look for this locket." He pulled out his watch and handed it over with the open locket to Bridger.

"I'll be danged," Bridger said. "This thing's been around. Last time I saw it, I handed it to that sea captain, Hogan. He said the fellas you shot on the road were a bad lot from off his ship.

He seemed glad to be shuck of them and promised to return the belongings to the men's kin. It was kinda odd how he looked at this thing, though, like he was surprised to see it."

Zac took the watch and caressed the open heart as he gazed at the flaxen-haired image of Jenny. Closing the locket, he threaded the chain through the buttonhole in his vest and dropped it into hiding. Then he studied Skip as he spun his top across the flagstones and laughed with Francisco.

"Seems to me that boy's an orphan because of a seagoing snake's jealousy," he said evenly. "And there's some mighty strange connection between ships, bankers, and desperados."

"And the railroad," Bridger added. "It's the one ingredient that mixes with the whole shebang."

"For whatever reason," Zac said, "he's in my keep now." The wiry agent pulled his pipe tobacco out of his vest and gently loaded it with a fresh mixture, pushing the grainy tobacco into the bowl. "You say opium was what I was hauling that morning?"

Bridger nodded silently.

"Well, it seems, then, I've got me a visit to pay on that warehouse where you say you saw it last."

He popped a flame onto the end of a match and puffed as he stuck it into the hole. "I'm doing something today I said I'd never do again. For the first time since the war, I'm buckling on an iron for me — not the company."

After filling their canteens with fresh, cold well

water, the three men said their goodbyes and started their horses across the brown, dry hills. Birds flitted over the tall, golden grass and Francisco tugged on his reins and spurred back down the hill for a last goodbye. He took off his black sombrero and waved it back and forth over his head.

"Adios, little amigo. You help Hans and stay out of trouble, you hear?"

They rode off with the sun at their backs, not watching, not knowing that they would be followed. While Hans worked in the kitchen the boy watched them disappear, then quietly mounted the little sorrel he had rode in on the day before.

The ride to the Cambria road meandered over the golden hills where the heat of the morning was already beating down on the dry grass. The three riders broke into a canter as their fresh horses seemed eager for the exercise. Bridger's stud maintained the pace, in spite of the fact that his day was already six hours old.

"I figure we're bound to have our hands full, looking into that merchantman at Moro, but that's where we gotta start," Bridger said.

Zachary said little. He set his jaw like a flint and turned his eyes toward the horizon, seeming to strain for the sight of the sea. He'd traveled this area many times before and was lost in his thinking. Unconcerned about what was around him, he put his spurs to the mare and galloped ahead.

"Sí, Señor Bridger. But you are such a big man. These sailor mans will not give us too much trouble, I think," Francisco shouted into the breeze.

Had any of the three been looking anywhere but between their horse's ears, they might have had a chance at spotting the hired guns who waited for them on their path that morning. It would have been difficult, though. These were professionals. They had killed men by stealth before and had little compunction about doing so. They knew their trade. They were separated, and stationed themselves on either side of the trail to hit their unsuspecting quarry from both sides.

The men's horses had been picketed out of sight, behind a hill. The red-headed first mate of the *Blue Goose* was standing by the horses. He had met the men who claimed to be special detectives for the railroad and ridden out with them to be certain they found the right road. O'Brien had assured them they could depend on him — he was the railroad man's brother.

Hal Jensen and Dirk Sims were known men who anchored the quartet. Hal was a bear of a man with flowing blond hair and a violent temper. He'd been known to kill anyone for a price and a number of men for just crossing him. Dirk was a crafty backshooter whose specialty was a Sharps at long distance. To him, a man in his sights was just a target, not a living, breathing human being.

The gunmen had worked out their ambush strategy well. Dirk had taken Mace Bishop and had staked out two clumps of oak trees on either side of the trail to the Cobb ranch. They would let the men pass, keeping their quarry in their sights. The gunfire up ahead from Hal and George Jefferies, a railroad detective without scruples, would be their signal to cut loose. Hal and George would hold their fire till it looked like they had the sheriff and his traveling companion pinned in between their sights on the trail, then they would release their deadly discharge.

That would be the signal for Dirk and Mace to squeeze off their triggers. Dirk was sure of a kill with a rider moving away from him. It was the easiest kind of shot.

He had climbed one of the oaks to get a better look up the trail. Being surprised was something he didn't like. He wanted to be ready. O'Brien had laid it out pretty well. The map had taken them to the right spot, and the manager had assured them that there would be two men on the trail that morning. The sheriff was the big one, and Dirk was assigned to kill the dark-haired one. They were to let the sheriff pass on the way in, and O'Brien swore Dirk's target would accompany Bridger on the way out. "When he hears a certain someone is missing, he'll come. You can be sure of that," he'd said.

CHAPTER 17

The assassins had long since poured water on their coffee fire. They didn't want to risk a blaze or the smell of smoke alerting their prey. Dirk looked down at the soaked coals from his vantage point high in the oak. He swung his head around, constantly surveying not only the trail leading to the ranch but the one that stretched behind them to the Cambria road. No sense being taken unawares. He knew this would be over right quick. They'd put some windows in these boys' skulls and be back in town long before supper, but he still didn't cotton to any surprises.

He expected to spot the men at a distance, but he saw the dust long before he saw the riders. "I see them, Mace," he shouted across the trail. "Gotta be more than two, though, and it looks like they're coming fast. That's gonna change things a might. Won't be so easy. Maybe we shoulda had our red-headed sailor boy join us in the shoot instead of holding the horses."

"I do believe his tool is a knife," Mace said. The big black buffalo soldier on the ground took out a handkerchief. He gave the signal to the men up the trail, and waited for the response, just like he'd been told to do. Seeing their return signal, he turned and worked the lever on his Winchester, sliding a shell into the chamber. He wiped his sweaty brow with the oily handkerchief and sank to his haunches behind the tree to wait it out. This wasn't his preferred way to kill a man, but money was money.

Mace had been in the war and stayed in the Army for several years afterward, but being a peacetime soldier never agreed with him. His specialty had been hand-to-hand fighting, and he liked to kill up close with a knife. There was something about watching the life rush out of a man up close that had a special thrill to him. He'd killed two soldiers in a fight at Hays City and it made him into a running deserter; but to the railroad, he was a valuable employee.

His imposing figure and the gleam in his eye at the thought of a fight seemed to put a quick end to any labor dispute. He practiced sighting down the barrel, grumbling inside at the thought of just passively standing behind a tree and shooting someone. He'd just as soon stop them on the road and kill them manly like. But he'd wait and he wouldn't miss.

The horses Zac's men rode were strong, and Zac was in a hurry to investigate the ship in the bay before high tide. It didn't belong there, unless it had something to hide. Zac had spurred his dun ahead of the other two and was determined to make the main road before slowing the mare down. Bridger's big roan kept up the pace well, and in spite of the long ride out in the early morning, Bridger was letting the little boy inside him enjoy the race to the sea. Francisco was atop a Morgan that genuinely looked out of place in the West. It came from his own father's stock and carried him well. He was too easygoing to allow himself to be caught up with this race to the road, but he followed close behind, keeping several lengths to the rear of Bridger's roan.

The three men had broken into a gallop with a dust cloud following them when they sped by the oak trees. Both Dirk and Mace were having trouble picking their targets out of the swirling dust when they heard the reports from the guns up ahead. They each picked up a dark shape through the dusty debris and, boxing their sights on the figures on horseback, let loose with two loud booms. Two men were knocked from their horses, and through the dust, Dirk could make out the third stop and kneel beside his fallen companions.

While Dirk reloaded his Sharps, Mace and the two up ahead continued to sight and fire at the one lone figure. The man was not returning their fire, however. He was flinging one of his fallen companions onto his horse while the other man, looking badly wounded, was remounting. *Those animals have obviously been well trained*, Dirk thought. When the saddles were empty, the horses stopped and returned to their fallen riders. While reloading and sighting through the dusky swirl, Dirk couldn't help but admire these men and the way they cared for their horseflesh.

"Zac, man, you okay? Let's get out of here.

They're not quitting out there."

"Yeah, I'll make it. Let's us get up the hill to those cottonwoods. There's a running spring up there and we can hunker down. How's Francisco?"

"Bad, Zac. Chest wound. I got him on his horse, though. Let's git!"

Dirk had spotted the dark-haired rider who was to be his key target. The man had seemed to be wounded by the first volley but had remounted and was holding the reins.

Dirk's sight squarely framed the man's back as his finger touched off the new load. Past his barrel, he could see the devastating impact of the bullet as it ripped into its target, launching the man forward and almost out of the saddle.

"Uh." Zac pitched forward as he gripped his oversized saddle horn. He felt like someone had thrown a cannonball squarely into his spine. He'd heard a sickening sound with the impact of the slug that hit him and wondered if this was it. The pain was overpowering. As the mare galloped up the hill, he held on with what little strength he had left.

His thoughts were abuzz. He'd faced death many times and always considered it just the last part of life. But he'd never had anyone depending on him before, and now thoughts of Jenny in trouble and a boy, already an orphan, made him desperately want to live, want to breathe. Through the pain, he tried to suck air into his lungs.

The three panic-stricken horses with their

beaten and semiconscious riders tore at the dry ground as they climbed the hill toward the cottonwood stand. They splashed through the entrails of the leaking spring atop the hill, as round after round spat at the ground or buzzed past them. At the top of the mound, Bridger pulled up the reins of his roan and the two horses he was tethering. He quickly scrambled to the ground and pulled the other two men flat onto the dry turf.

"Zac, Zac, you all right?"

"I don't know . . . I hurt mighty terrible. My back. Where's Francisco? How bad is he?"

The bullets continued to sing through the air, with occasional rounds from the Sharps coming perilously close to the men lying on the ground.

"Francisco looks bad, Zac. He took a shot straight on through the brisket. I don't think he's gonna make it."

"I've got to get to him, Jeff. Where is he?"

"Lie still, man. I'm going to drag you back a might before that Sharps walks right in on us."

Dirt kicked up into their faces from the rifle fire below, and as Bridger hunkered lower to the ground, he began to slowly pull Zac a few yards toward the top of the mound. He watched the puffs of smoke from below and winced as he followed what he thought were the trajectories of the slugs sent their way.

"You caught a clean one through the shoulder, Zachary. Just got the meat. Don't think it broke a bone."

Zac closed his eyes and ground his teeth. Opening them with a familiar twinkle, he said, "I don't get it. How can they hit us and miss somebody as big as you?"

"Maybe with this star they were afraid to hit me," Bridger said. "You know how the law is respected around here."

"I sure do," said Zac.

"I only see blood pumping out of your shoulder," said Bridger. "Nothing seems to be pooling up under your back." The sheriff stuffed a handkerchief into the bleeding shoulder wound. "Brace yourself," Bridger said. "I'm gonna try to turn you over."

Bridger scooted his arms under Zac's back and began a slow, even turn. "I'll be danged," he said. "I never saw the like."

With that, the sheriff unbuckled one of Zac's ammunition bandoleers and, unslinging it from around his friend's shoulder, held up a prize trophy. "Did you ever see such?" Bridger said. The big slug from the Sharps had fused into one of the lead cartridges looped through the back of the belt. Bridger lifted Cobb's shirt to get a better look. "You're going to have one heap of a bruise. But I'll wager that's all it'll be."

The shooting had stopped from below, and in their moment of discovery the silence had gone unnoticed. "They're going for position," Zac said. "I've got to get to Francisco."

He carefully crawled over to the dying man on the hill and removed Francisco's hat. "Eees bad, Señor Zac, no?"

"Yes, compadre. I won't lie to you. You'll go no farther than here."

"You go, mi amigo. Give me my gun and you and the sheriff fly away while you can."

A shot from the big buffalo killer below bounced dust off the hat in Zac's right hand. He scrambled to lie prone at Francisco's side. "I don't know, my friend. They're going for better position. My guess is they'll try to keep us pinned down and loft some shoulder artillery up here for a while. Who knows."

Francisco grabbed Zac's hand and squeezed it tight. "Señor Zac, you gonna have to get out of this. You got to take care of little Skip. Everybody he loves is dead but you, señor. It is too sad a thing to be alive when everyone you love is dead."

Zac hung his head a little and lifted his eyes into Francisco's. "That's the way I've been living since the war, Francisco. I've made it; he'll make it."

"No, no, Señor Zac. You only think so. You love many people and they love you. You love the sheriff, you love Miss Jenny, you love little Skip now, and, Señor Zac, I think you even love me. Only, you too locked up inside to see all those around you."

A smile crossed Francisco's lips as he said, "You even love that mean old cook, Hans. Nobody else could, not even his mama." A laugh brought a cough of blood to the Mexican's mouth. It trickled down the sides of his cheek.

"Take care of little Skip, give him a home. You love him, señor."

The last breath passed through Francisco's lips, and as Zac gently closed his eyes, Bridger began firing down the hill with his rifle. "They're circling around," he said. "I'd say we're in deep trouble. I see three of them moving for position among them oaks in front, but I'd swear there was a fourth. Where is he?"

Just then Zac sniffed at the breeze blowing in from the west, a strong wind behind them. "You smell that?" he asked.

Bridger swung his head around from the sights of his Winchester. "Smoke!" he said. He inched toward the edge of the hill and rolled toward the cottonwood trees. The spring that still bubbled up from the crest of the hill cut into the hillside and offered him a slight depression and an opportunity to lower his considerable profile.

While Zac exchanged shots on the opposite side with the three men firing from the bottom of the slope, the sheriff removed his hat and peered down the hill in the direction of the smoke. He watched a tall man in a derby move from one section of dry grass to another, torch in hand.

The man swiftly rolled the blazing torch over the top of the dry grass as the wind from the sea started to sweep the undergrowth into a torrent of flame. Bridger looked all around the surface of the hill and took stock of the tall, dry vegetation that covered the ground as far as he could see. Parts of the hill were so tall in crisp grasses that he knew they came up to his chest. Bridger also knew the wind, combined with the slope of the hill, would turn their position into a blazing inferno in a matter of minutes.

The man in the derby continued his busy work of death at a position out of effective rifle range, but that was not going to stop Bridger from taking a chance. He worked the lever on his Winchester, rammed a cartridge into the chamber, and lifted the rear sights. Taking a careful look at the man below, he positioned his windage sight and tightened his finger on the trigger. Relaxing his muscles, Bridger waited for the man below to pause and admire his work. He had hunted often, and many times would stop and wait for a bounding deer to pause at the edge of a hill and take that one last look backward that would spell its doom.

Suddenly it happened! The man stopped and stretched to full height, watching with pride as the flames raced toward the slope of the hill. Bridger exhaled very slightly and squeezed the trigger. The shot's trajectory rose and plunged toward its target, slamming squarely into the railroad detective's upper thigh. He dropped to the ground like a chicken taken out with an axe. Beginning to roll on the ground, the tall stranger howled in pain as blood from an artery soaked the ground. Bridger rose slightly and started toward Zac, sprinting with rifle in hand.

"We got to move. We ain't got much time." Bridger dropped to the ground, throwing his hat aside.

The bushwhackers below had taken good shooting positions, and with the fire set on three sides of the hill, they were ready to put down a murderous crossfire into the one avenue of escape. They held their fire, watching the flames begin their roaring ascent up the grassy slope. They were going to be mighty sure their rifles weren't empty when the men on top came running for their lives.

"Jeff, they've got good position down there," Zac said. "They're behind those trees in a prime spot to triangulate. They'll bust our britches good if we ride down that way."

"One thing's for sure," Bridger said. "If we stay here — we'll fry!"

"Some things are for sure, but that ain't one of them," Zac said. "Come on, let's get to the horses."

Jeff Bridger had learned about men who had their minds made up. There was no sense reasoning with them. In most cases such a man could be dangerous, but with Zachary Taylor Cobb there was a difference. He was someone who thought things through and always had the odds figured. He was hell on wheels at a poker table; but to Zac, poker was just practice for the business of living. He was cool all the time, even on a hill about to burst into flame.

Zac began stripping the saddles from the horses and Bridger followed suit without question. At a time like this, Bridger knew that he had to trust Zac in whatever the man had in mind. The panic-stricken horses had caught the smell of smoke and their nostrils flared wildly at the breeze. Zac pulled up the deep-set picket pins. He swung his hat and with a swift slap to their hindquarters, sent the animals plunging down the hill.

"Jeff, you grab Francisco. I'll take the rifles and blankets." With that, the two men gathered what they could and scurried through the grass toward the smoke, the oncoming wall of flame, and the trickling spring. "We've got to make it to the spring before the flames do," Zac shouted. The smoke was billowing, with dark columns rising. Both Zac and the sheriff drew their bandannas over their noses as they raced through the tall grass. They reached the spring, and Zac tossed the blankets into the flat, flowing seepage.

He knelt down and spread the blankets into the flow. "Lay down in this, Jeff. You may not get enough of you wet to make that much of a difference, but every drop'll help." The two men rolled in the soaked blankets, then they cradled their rifles and stared through the smoke at the oncoming wall of flame. Showers of sparks and soot blew into their covered faces.

Zac soaked his hat as best he could and pulled it low over his ears. Both men lay in the trickle of water and pulled the blankets up over the top of them. They listened to the roar of the flames and felt the warm steam pouring off of their blankets. What a moment before had been a peaceful hillside, filled with flowers, tall grass, and buzzing bees, was now a blazing hell on earth. It ripped over the steaming men as both lay praying for it to pass. Zac placed his face directly into what little water lay under him and held his breath.

CHAPTER 18

Skip felt exposed. It seemed to him that no matter what he did, he would wind up anxiously twisting inside, wondering what would become of him, where he would live, who he would be with. Over the last few weeks he'd learned to exist with the feeling of fear creeping through his insides. He'd been too numb to feel it as he stood over his father's hastily dug grave on the stage road that night. But since then, the gnawing question of what was to happen to him had been digging away in his stomach.

As he rode the trail to the sea from the hacienda, he took out his father's watch and opened it up to look at the happy picture of a family that no longer existed. He'd been just a baby in the picture. Gazing at it, he wanted to go back in time somehow and warn the little child being held in his mother's arms what lay ahead in life, but he couldn't. There was no turning back.

He knew he couldn't help now, if there was any trouble; still, he wanted to be with Zac and Francisco — to try. It made him shudder to remember the night in the dark cave when he had to fire the shotgun that took a man's life. He didn't think he could ever do that again, no matter who the man was. Life had become too precious to Skip and too fragile. Because of these feelings, he felt protective and he was afraid to be alone. He trotted the sorrel in an easy manner, not wanting to overtake the men he was pursuing. Turning to the watch to take a last look at the picture, he heard the first two shots boom in the distance. He snapped his head upright and heard two more.

Skip cantered the sorrel ahead while listening to what sounded like a small war. He continued to move the pony forward and considered it a good sign that the shooting hadn't stopped. Within minutes he saw the first smoke; he could still hear sporadic gunfire, and something else . . . "Boy . . . Boy . . . Stop. . . . Go no farther." Skip wheeled around to see a springboard rig bouncing along the road in the distance. Like a squirrel in a cage, Hans, the cook from the ranch, was swinging a whip in the air and driving the rig at top speed, his white apron still clinging to his sides. Skip could make out the classic gray muttonchop whiskers even at a distance. He froze his pony, then moved alongside the road. This was an old man he didn't want to cross.

The rig slid to a running stop with Hans rising in his seat and heaving at the reins. The horses slung their heads to the side and rose up in the harness, so great was the pull of the old man now standing in the seat. Skip could see from the lather that streaked their coats that they'd been driven hard. "Herr Bond," the old man said, "you have made me much concern." The stiffness and formality in the old man's voice was typical of Hans.

Suddenly, they both looked up the road, mesmerized at the sight of three riderless horses without saddles charging toward them. Both recognized Zac's mare at first glance, the blaze running down her forehead. The animals turned aside from the road but continued past the startled onlookers, maintaining the direction of the ranch. "Boy, you get those horses and come back here. I'll go up ahead and see vot I can do."

The balding, whiskered cook slid his Spencer carbine from under the seat, planted his feet, and swung the whip over the ears of the team. They bolted in the direction of the smoke, dragging the springboard after them.

Zac lay under the smoky blanket, almost afraid to move a muscle. He could still hear the flames roaring, yet they seemed to have passed their location. Slinging aside the edge of the blanket, he sat up, blinked back smoky tears and stared at the flickering rubble all around him. He could see the flames leaping at the edge of the hill. He saw small flames smoldering on the fabric of Bridger's blanket and threw his own blanket over the sheriff's to smother what remained.

"Jeff, Jeff, you all right?" He shook his unconscious friend, then turned him over. One look sent Zac into a panic. Bridger was unconscious. He put his ear to the massive chest and could hear no heartbeat. He lifted him off the ground and slammed him back into the dirt, something he'd seen done once during the war. No effect. Again he slammed Bridger into the ground.

"Hawmph . . ." Bridger sputtered and coughed repeatedly. Finally, he opened his eyes. "What happened?" he sputtered, rolling over onto his back and crossing his arms over his chest to steady the pain. "What in tarnation happened?"

"The good Lord pulled your bacon out of the fire, my friend." Bridger blinked at Zac and continued to cough. Zac offered him a nearby canteen. "Take some of this. How do you feel?"

"Like my insides have been dragged and stomped on by a horse."

Zac stroked his chin and mused, "My mama used to say that if a body kept faithful, he wouldn't go into the fire. Come to think of it, though, she did say you'd go through it a few times."

"Well, I'd durn sure say what just went over us made up for going through the flames more than a few times," Bridger responded.

Both of the men noticed the wind shift at the same time. The smoke was now blowing back toward them. Zac spoke up, " 'Bout this time every day in the summer, we get the winds from the valley."

"Well," said Bridger, "that'll help you boys out on this side of Cambria. That fire won't go nowhere coming back this way. Nothing left to burn. But the smoke in our eyes ain't gonna make it easier to see those fellas with the rifles down there," Bridger said.

Zac mopped his forehead. "When those horses of ours make it back to the ranch, it ought to stir something up."

Bridger checked the loads in his Colt sidearm. "Well, if I was them down there," he nodded in the direction of the slope, "I'd figure us to be a couple of hams set up for the winter by now and just ride off."

Then they heard the shots below. In rapid succession, they blasted away, followed by what appeared to be yelling and cursing. Zac smiled and scrambled to his feet. "I'd recognize the sound of that Spencer anywhere. It's Hans. And that raspy voice — he sounds like he's swearing a blue streak when he wants you to pass the salt."

With rifles in hand they both sprinted to the eclipse of the hill. Stooping low, they stopped and peered through the smoke. Below them lay the blond on the ground and Hans with leveled rifle pointed at the big black man. In the distance they could see two men on horseback riding hell-bent for leather in the direction of Moro Bay. One was bareheaded and had long, flaming red hair and a beard.

Zac squinted in recognition of the fleeing form and pointed. "I've seen that backside before. I'd bet dollars to your horseshoe nails that he's the one that got away on the road to town. I owe him and I've seen enough of his backside. I'll see him face-to-face before this day's over." They

210

moved through the smoke and ran down the blackened hill.

"I come over ze hill und I start to shoot," Hans said. "Ze blond over there, him I got with the first shot and the vay the feller with the buffalo gun took off, he must have thought ze whole Prussian cavalry vas behind me. But zis big fella," Hans pointed to the ex-buffalo soldier, "he stopped and wanted to fight. More spine than sense, zis one has."

Bridger walked over to where the man was sitting. "You want to tell me who you are and why you're shooting at us?"

"My name's Mace and the rest is my own business."

"Well, Mace, I'm Sheriff Jeff Bridger. I don't know who you are, but I do know there's a fine man up on that hill dead because of you. We'll just have to see if your memory comes back at the trial."

Then Zac stepped up to the big man and said, "What do you know about Jenny Hays? Where is she?"

"Man, I don't know nothing about no woman." He rose up from his sitting position and started to move toward Zac. "You ain't the bossman and I don't have to tell you nothing. 'Sides, if'n I'd a had it my way, I wouldn't have used no gun. I'd a tore your pretty head clean off." He leaned in Zac's direction and the sheriff pushed Cobb away.

"Zac, I'm the law here. You've got to let me

handle this my own way." Suddenly, the sheriff rushed his left fist across his body and delivered a crashing blow to the big assassin's chin. Bridger put his hands on his hips and stared at the suddenly prone man. "Somehow I can just tell that there's only one way to reason with you and get the answers we want."

The big man slowly rose to his feet and dusted off the backside of his trousers. Speaking through smiling white teeth, he drawled, "That's right, Mr. Sheriff. If'n you can whup me I'll tell you anything you wants to hear."

With that, he circled Bridger as the sheriff pulled off his shirt. "If this thing gets torn," Bridger said, "what my Mrs. will do to me will make this event look like patty-cake."

The railroad thug put his head down and charged like a bull elk, but Bridger deftly stepped aside to his right and sent a downward punch into the side of the passing man's head. Down now on all fours, the man slowly began to rise up and look around. "You move right smart for such a big man, Sheriff."

Bridger held up both fists. "I put in a spell in the gold fields, boxing. These scars you see on my face are war badges. I've seen many a braying bull like you taken down."

With that, Bridger moved swiftly to his left in a circle around the railroad man, bouncing a series of left jabs off the man's jaw. With each blow the man's head was snapped back by the force of Bridger's fist. "Slap! Slap! Whap!" The repeated punishment came with catlike quickness. All at once, the sheriff swung a hard right into the big man's midsection. The whoosh of air could be clearly heard as the railroad bully dropped to his knees. Bridger leaned over the man's head. "Had enough?" he asked.

Suddenly the man's head came up sharply, cracking Bridger on the chin. The bully sprang to his feet and planted a bruising blow to the sheriff's jaw. Then with brute force he lofted a punch into Bridger's midsection. "Sheriff, you is a big tough man. I can see why you is the sheriff." He crashed a roundhouse into Bridger's jaw as he spoke that sent the lawman to the ground. "Nobody's stood up to me the way you has, but now I'm a gonna whup you like a child." With that he stepped forward and sent a massive kick into Bridger's prone body.

Stepping back, he sized up his target for another bashing kick. But as he swung his foot forward, Bridger caught the tip of his boot with a quickness and sure grip that didn't seem possible. Rising up to a sitting position, the sheriff held the big man's foot with both hands and seemed to balance him, then he twisted the ankle out with deliberate strength. "Snap." The sound of the popping ankle bones signaled an end to the contest.

"Ow! Blast you! You done broke my ankle!"

Zac reached out and gave his hand to the sheriff to help him up. He turned his attention to the man in pain on the ground. "We'll get you patched up," Zac said. "You may have to get up the gallows on crutches, but we'll see you get up there."

The hired gun dropped his hand from his injured joint to the other leg. Slipping his fingers into his boot, he felt for his knife. In an easy motion he slid it up the boot and grabbed the blade, cocking his arm to throw. But Bridger was not taken by surprise. He moved forward and kicked the weapon, spinning it away from the wounded man. "None of that!" he shouted. "I need you alive to tell us what we want to know. And if you'd a tried to throw that knife, my friend here woulda killed you. Lord knows he's got enough reason already."

Zac had drawn his Colt, and soberly looked the big man in the eye as he returned the pistol to his holster.

"Now, you may not like it," Bridger added, "but you're whipped and you owe us some answers."

The man grimaced in pain. "Yep, I reckon I does at that. Ya'll done beat me fair and square, even if you done broke my leg." He stopped and tried to straighten his injured limb. He gritted his teeth and let out a whistle followed by several short but shrill breaths through his teeth. "That woman ya'll is looking for; I ain't seen her, but I figure to know where she is." He went on, "Truth is, the manager at the end of the track —"

Bridger interrupted, "You mean O'Brien?"

"Yeah, shore 'nuff. That was his name. He told

us to go to a ship in Moro Bay today when the job was done. We was to get paid there by the captain. He gave us a map here, but said his brother was to meet us on the road near the bay and would take us here. Fact is, he was holdin' our horses. Guess he done lit out with Dirk when the old man showed up. We wasn't expecting someone to flank us from the rear. Damnation, that old man can shoot!"

Hans put down the blanket he'd been using to beat out the dying flames along the rim of the hill and spoke up. "I received ze very best training from ze students of Frederick ze Great. I keep to ze firing position and never let up until ze enemy is down or has fled ze field." With that Hans slapped his heels together. Zac and Jeff watched him beam with pride, and for a moment were afraid he would insist on a hero's parade.

Mace went on, "Fitz, the manager's brother, said something about a woman they had. They all seemed to believe that would bring your friend" — he nodded in the direction of Zac — "back down the road with you. Seems the captain was especially concerned about getting him laid out." The men all looked at one another with a puzzled look. "By the way," Mace asked with a clever look at Zac, "you got yourself a gold locket on you?"

Zac took out his watch and held the chain up to the black man's eyes. "You mean this?" he asked.

"Yeah, that's it. I guess the captain of that ship

215

sets a powerful store in that piece 'o gold. Fitz claims it got stolen by one of the crew and he's been after it ever since."

Zac looked at Bridger and said, "That would be one of those men brought in from the road. Must have been doing a little sneak thief work for himself."

Mace looked up. "That's really all I know. I generally like to know why I'm killing somebody that ain't done nothing to me, but it's not something I has to have. The only thing I has to have is the money."

Hanging on the black man's words, neither Zac nor Bridger heard the horses that pounded up the trail behind a lone rider. Skip reined his mount in front of the men, the three bareback horses tethered behind him. He wasted no time dismounting and running to Zac. "I-I-I know I sh-sh-sh . . . shouldn't have followed you. I w-w-w . . . was skeered."

Hans stood beside the boy and put a hand on his shoulder. "I know that zis is not my business and I do believe in following orders, but if zis lad had not followed you and made me to chase after him, I would not have seen the smoke nor heard ze shots and you vould be still up zere on ze hill."

Zac dropped to one knee in front of the boy and, putting his arms around him, pulled him tightly to his chest. He kept hugging him while trying to think of how to break the news that Francisco was gone. "Skip, you remember me telling you about my mother and what she said about how God uses our ma and pa?" He pushed the boy to arm's length, keeping a grip on the lad's shoulders.

The little boy nodded. "Y-Y-Y . . . Yes, sir. She s-s-s . . . said God uses them as His hands, a-a-a . . . arms, and eyes on this earth. Yes, I do r-r-r . . . remember."

"Well, you're special Skip, and God has used other people in your life to do that as well."

The boy swiveled his head, looking for Francisco, then turned back to Zac. Tears started to fall. It was as if he knew what was coming next.

"Well, son, one of those people God used for you is gone." The tears cascaded down Skip's face and his blinking couldn't stop them.

Zac turned his head from the boy and looked at the men who silently listened. Turning back to the tearful boy, he said, "Skip, the last words Francisco said to me were about taking care of you and loving you. He was thinking of you at the very last. And" — Zac dipped his head and spoke in a softer tone — "I've got something else to tell you. Even when I was being shot at moving up that hill, all I could think about was coming home to you. I've never had thoughts like that before."

Zac watched as the little boy continued to cry. But the child's attention never strayed from Zac or his words. And though Zac didn't know exactly how to say it — he'd never told anyone before that he loved them — he wanted to tell Skip that he was going to take care of him, make him feel

217

like he was home, that he belonged. He just didn't know how to put the words into the feeling. "Skip, you're clearing out a spot in my life and I'm gonna make sure you stay there; you understand that, son?"

The boy slowly nodded, then lunged at Zac, squeezing him tightly around the neck. "I love you, Zac."

CHAPTER 19

Jenny had listened to the barrels of water and boxes of provisions being loaded all day. The creaking of the winches and the shouts of the crew to the longboats had kept her on edge. It was obvious this ship was being prepared for a long voyage and she didn't want to be on it. The gold strikes in the Sierras had also depleted the crew, so fresh hands were being gathered from a stingy, shrinking source of local manpower.

Jenny got the idea from listening at her door and at the porthole that not all the new crew members were conscious when they came aboard. And with each hour that passed, she could tell that Captain Hogan was growing more impatient with the drawn-out preparations. His shouts to the crew were becoming impassioned and salty.

"Hogan, Captain Michael Hogan!" She pounded on the door with her clenched fists. Overhearing his voice below deck only moments before, she knew he could hear her now. She knew that in all likelihood the captain's presence would mean only another argument and would not result in her release, yet her patience was wearing thin and simply the presence of another human being would be a welcome change.

"Open this door immediately!" she shouted. "I

demand to be allowed off this ship at once." She pressed her lips to the bulkhead door and, emotionally exhausted, rolled her cheek and ear onto the door's surface. She heard the lock begin to slide and stood back away from the door. Gently, it swung open.

"My dear, I know you're upset, so I've brought you some brandy to calm you down." The captain steered a silver tray with two large glasses and an ornate cut-glass decanter onto Jenny's bedside table.

"Upset! I'm more than upset." Jenny rose to her feet and, rounding the table, moved toward the captain, her arms rigid at her sides. "I'm being kidnapped! I don't know what they do to men who do such things in your part of the world, Captain, but the men in this area will leave you looking through the cottonwood trees on the end of a rope."

"Dear Jenny, you are being a might harsh, aren't you? I'm merely offering you the protection of my vessel." He took the decanter and poured two liberal glasses of the thick liquid. Striking a match, he lit the candle on the table beside the tray. "I always prefer my spirits heated," he said. "It fills the nose and floods the soul, not just the stomach." He held the edge of the glass near the open candle flame.

Jenny's eyes were red and the fatigue she felt was telling on her. Her head drooped down and she caught sight of her dress. "Look at this dress, it's been torn!" She lifted up a tattered sleeve. "I will need something to sew it back together with."

The captain continued to silently stare into the flame that was heating the half-full glass. "You'll enjoy this Napoleon, my dear, very fine and very old; and just as the flame brings out the full flavor, so the brandy does to the one who drinks it."

Jenny caught herself. Her mind had been drifting; she was exhausted. A surge of anger suddenly erupted in her eyes. "You may take your liquor any way you please, Captain! I prefer to choose my own partners to drink with, however; and it won't be you!"

"I'm sorry to hear that, my dear."

Jenny froze on the edge of the bed as the captain ran the back of his hand down the length of her dress. "In my area of the world, white women are a valued commodity. They are taken to quite a number of places and sold for amazing sums of money. Men of the Far East consider white women quite a delicacy, you see. Someone like you might make this voyage very profitable."

A smile crossed his lips, showing pearly teeth beneath his brown moustache. "In such places where these women are sold, they drink with many men." With a curling smile, he lifted his eyes from her dress and looked into hers as he held up the heated brandy to his nose. "Of course as my wife, you would be given protection and every courtesy. The money would be hard to pass by, but with you as compensation . . ."

Jenny wanted to maintain a facade of control, but she shivered at such a thought and her shoulders twitched in a way that displayed her disgust and fear.

"Captain!" Both Jenny and Hogan turned to the open door, where a man with red hair and a flaming beard had suddenly appeared. His green eyes met Jenny's and seemed to burn a message into her memory, a message she couldn't understand, couldn't remember. "Captain, something has happened and I need to see you at once and explain it." The man's face looked flushed and perspiration beaded up on his high forehead. For a moment Jenny thought Hogan's face seemed to turn color as well. Instead, he maintained his composure and turned to Jenny.

"Please excuse me, Miss Hays. There's a matter I must attend to. Please continue to enjoy the hospitality of the *Blue Swan*. Meanwhile, I will have the steward bring you something to sew with." She thought it strange that Hogan had slipped and called his ship by the name of her dead fiance's vessel, but the captain's distracted look told her that something in his plan had gone very, very wrong. He hurried out the door behind the man with the red beard and, closing the door behind him, slid the lock on the outside firmly into place.

Zac rode the mare hard into Cambria, clattering down the street and out toward the direction of the dock and the pots of boiling blubber. He'd been taken advantage of by Race Talbot. All during the fast ride to Cambria his mind had rehearsed the uninvited burdens he now carried because of that simple favor. He'd carried the man's whale oil into San Luis, never knowing he was really transporting opium for the Tong. How could he have known the other side of the dispute would try to hijack his cargo? Brooding, he thought, *Now I'm the enemy of the railroad. They tried to kill me, they did kill Francisco, Jenny's missing, and now, by God . . . somebody has to pay!* Zac was determined to start collecting with Race Talbot.

He skidded the mare to a running stop in the sand outside the pot shack. With the fresh wound in his left shoulder, Zac couldn't do to Race what he'd like to, but he'd durn sure put the fear of God into him and maybe more. He swung himself to the ground and, reaching into his saddlebags, drew out the sawed-off shotgun and crammed some extra shells into his pocket.

"Race!" he shouted. "Race Talbot!" With that, he kicked open the door that hid the office.

Several burly seamen were gathered around a table drinking coffee, and Talbot rose up from the end of it and stepped toward the side, smiling like he was seeing a long-lost cousin. "Hey, Zachary, me boy, come and have some java with us here."

Zac transferred the shotgun to his left hand and without breaking stride stormed across the room. Ramming his right arm under Talbot's chin, he drove him into the wall. "You double-crossing four flusher. Why didn't you tell me I was carrying opium in that oil of yours?"

Talbot croaked out a response from behind Zac's arm. "I didn't want to involve you, Zac."

"Well, you did involve me, you son of a mangy cur. You got a good friend of mine killed and another one kidnapped." Zac used his thumb to cock the hammers on the shotgun. The pain in his left shoulder even from this minor effort had left him throbbing; the hard ride had opened up his wound.

Talbot swallowed hard. "You're bleeding, lad, let me help you."

Zac placed the shotgun barrels next to the frightened man's throbbing temple. "Oh, you're going to help me, all right, or these friends of yours will be scrubbing your brains off this wall."

"Sure, boy, sure. Anything you want. I'm just a businessman here." He edged his head around under Zac's death lock and looked at the men, who were now against the wall. "Aren't I, boys? Just a businessman. A simple sailor."

Zac buried the edges of the shotgun barrels slightly deeper into the man's temple. "Well, Mr. Sailor, you and I are going to take a little boat ride down the coast. We're going to use one of those stinking things you call a fishing boat and you're gonna be at the tiller." Releasing the man's Adam's apple from his forearm, he took Talbot's collar with his right hand and slung him toward the door. He then reached up on a shelf near the door and took several of the explosive charges used to fire harpoons. "We're gonna have a nice long talk about opium and the Chinese, and you'd better have a lot to say, or you can say goodbye to these friends of yours for good."

Dirk had scaled the ladder of the mercantile and positioned himself facing the street. He was counting on the news of O'Brien's whereabouts to reach the sheriff when he rode into town, and he knew the well-lit batwing doors of the Oriental would form the perfect target backdrop for the sheriff's large frame. He checked the load in his Sharps and took down the sight. The slight distance across the street was a shot even a child could make. He rolled a smoke and waited until he saw Bridger and Mace ride up to the jail down the street. He figured he'd take just one last smoke to relax, then he'd put it out and get ready to shoot.

Jeff Bridger had brought his prisoner all the way to San Luis. They had ridden the horses hard and pulled up outside the sheriff's office. Walking in behind the prisoner, Bridger saw his startled deputy. "Lock this one up. He helped to murder Zac Cobb's man Francisco. Durn near had me planted too."

While the deputy was in the back turning the key, Bridger opened a drawer and took out a box of shells. Thumbing fresh rounds into a shotgun, he watched the deputy hang the keys. "I'm gonna need to borrow that horse of yours. My roan's plumb spent and this day ain't nearly over yet," he said.

"How's that?" the deputy responded.

"Well, that prisoner of ours works for the railroad. Fact is, he's a hired killer of theirs, and I've got to go out to the end of the track and arrest the manager, O'Brien."

The deputy blinked and his eyes got big. "You won't have to do that, Jeff; he's in town. He's down to the Oriental, drinking."

Bridger froze for a moment, then continued to reload. "You see anybody else ride up lately?"

"Matter of fact, I did. 'Bout half hour ago when I was in the Oriental, a lean-looking gent rode up and come into the bar like he was searching for someone. I'd guess O'Brien was who he was looking for, 'cause he sauntered up to him at his table and just sat himself down."

"Yep," Bridger said, "that would be my other problem. He had a hand in the ambush on the road from Cobb's place. When Zac's old cook showed up, though, with that Spencer repeater, he lit out. Take yourself that scatter-gun on the rack and you go down and cover the back door. I'll go to the front."

With that, the two lawmen separated. Bridger left by way of the front door while his deputy scooted out the back and down the alleyway. The streets were dark now and the only lights were from the saloons and the jail.

Music floated through the night breeze, and Jeff could watch the smoke curl out the doors of the Oriental only a block away. His spurs made a rhythmic, musical reply to the sound of the piano as he swung his head from side to side.

He paused before the alley and quickly made his way to the other side of the walk. Peering into doorways, he maintained a careful look-see approach. He'd been told often enough that the only brave lawmen were dead now, and while he was perfectly willing to face trouble, he did not want to face it! He knew he presented an easy target for the worst of shots, and that he needed an even chance, if that was possible.

He glanced at the windows on the opposite side of the dark street, but could see only the reflected glare of the glass or darkness. He wasn't looking at the roof of each building, however, or he might have spotted the long barrel of the Sharps that was being walked the length of the street with him in its sights. A perfect pace was maintained between the muzzle of the weapon and Bridger's easy walk. Even now a shot would be fatal, but the assassin was waiting — waiting for the doors of the Oriental, waiting for the perfect kill.

Bridger stopped at the lathered horse in front of the saloon. It had been ridden hard and appeared to have been recently tied up outside. He ran his hand over the horse's withers to see if the sweat was dry or wet. It was fresh. Glancing along the side of the saddle, he could see the empty rifle boot. Whoever had ridden the animal in had taken his rifle with him. Jeff shrugged. *Maybe that isn't unusual at all,* he thought. He stared at the doors of the saloon and into the bright light pouring into the street.

Bridger stepped to the batwing doors and suddenly heard a shout from behind. Falling from the top of the roof was a rifle that bounced on the awning of the mercantile and landed on the walk with a thud. Bridger ran toward the fallen rifle and heard the struggle on top of the building. Running toward the alleyway on the side of the store, he spotted the ladder attached to the building. Jeff leaned the shotgun to the side of the building and swung his weight onto the ladder. His spurs rang out as he scaled it. Reaching the top, he drew his revolver and rolled over the edge of the building and onto the roof.

Toward the front of the building, he saw the form of a man on the roof in the shadows. His legs were bent and his arms were lying loosely by his side. Jeff cocked his revolver and, keeping low, scooted toward the fallen form. The man's eyes were glistening with tears and at a glance Bridger could see the huge slice across his neck. Blood was still flowing and a massive dark stain covered his shirt and was forming a pool at his side.

Suddenly, out of the corner of his eye, Jeff saw a flash. Only a shadow, it moved toward the side of the building and in an instant, before Jeff could draw a bead on it, it was gone!

Lying beside the dying man was a strange instrument. An ornamental hatchet wrapped in red cloth had been carefully laid down as some sort of calling card. Unwrapping the cloth, Jeff could see the picture of a dragon. *The Tong,* he thought. *My old unwanted highbinder friend.*

He picked up the hatchet and stepped back down the ladder to the alley below. Grabbing the shotgun, he made his way across the street.

The sheriff slowly walked through the batwing doors and stood at the entrance of the Oriental saloon. Tinny piano music ripped through the room as he surveyed the crowd.

There he is! Bridger walked toward one of the gambling tables in the back of the room and cocked both barrels on the big scatter-gun.

The red-haired rail boss spotted the lawman halfway across the room, and a look of surprise spread across his face. When Bridger walked up to the table, the stocky railroad man dropped his hand to his side.

Bridger carried the shotgun in the crook of his arm and lowered it to face the redbeard. "I wouldn't," he said. "Personally, you'd do me a favor if you went for a gun, and you'd save the taxpayers to boot." Bridger reached into his belt and pulled out the oriental hatchet. He dropped it on the table in the middle of a stack of poker chips. "Found that next to the body of your bush-whacker across the street." He looked the man straight in the eye. "Come to think of it, maybe you should go for that gun and do your own killing for a change."

The big Irishman stood up and held out his hands. "I'm just a businessman, Sheriff, trying to bring prosperity to your town." He looked around at the men at the table and then gingerly opened his coat, exposing a six-gun he was carrying. "You can have my weapon, Sheriff, then these men will all be able to testify to my defenselessness if I should turn up dead on the way to your jail."

"Oh, don't worry, you'll make it to my jail. I wouldn't want to miss the pleasure of seeing you behind bars."

"That may be, me bucko, but the railroad has some very fine attorneys, and you can be sure I'll be out of your jail first thing in the morning."

CHAPTER 20

Zac lay motionless on the deck of the little boat. The sail was full in a stiff offshore breeze as it carried him and Race Talbot down the coast toward Moro Bay. Zac's head was propped up against the rail and the pain in his neck from the uncomfortable position was serving to keep him awake. He held the shotgun loosely pointed in the direction of the frightened sailor.

"Look, lad, you've lost a lot of blood. You better let me turn this thing around. I'll take you to my house and have the missus nurse you. You really should be in bed."

Zac tore his shirt and wrapped it tightly around his shoulder. Gripping the cloth in his teeth, he tore it into long shreds. He placed the strips over the makeshift bandage and tightened the ends into hard knots.

"I've told you all I know, Zac. I know what I did in involving you was wrong, but I just didn't think the railroad knew where the shipments were coming from. I can tell you one thing, though, that Chinese bunch knows everything there is to know. They ain't as dumb as a body might think."

"Your opium operation is your own concern, Talbot. You get mixed up with these people, and you'll be wearing a knife in your spine before you

231

know it. My concern right now is just Jenny. I've got to get on board that ship and get her off it."

"The tide'll be full within a couple of hours, me boy. That'll be the time they'll be steering that clipper out of there. Problem is, I don't think you can even climb a rope ladder in the condition you're in, much less carry on a rescue against an armed ship's crew."

"You let me take care of that problem, Talbot. All I want you to do is get me to that channel."

Moro Rock's massive structure loomed in the distance, a giant sculpture built by the fingers of God. Its beauty and size seemed out of place to the rest of the shoreline and concealed a small channel and the tiny harbor of Moro Bay. Magellan himself had dropped anchor in this hidden cove years before. With the plan that Zac had in mind, he wanted to make sure the black clipper that now lay at anchor wouldn't reach the open sea.

Even if he couldn't stop the crew and the captain, he was determined to make sailing out of Moro Bay a very dangerous business for them. If he could block the entrance to the harbor, then help could arrive. Surely Bridger would arrange a posse to come to the ship and rescue Jenny as soon as he was able. There was also no telling what else they might find.

The captain tightened the halyard and the boat began to heave to. With the offshore breeze, the little vessel was running south on a broad reach, with Talbot struggling at the wheel, leaning on it to hold the boat on a straight course. The approaching night sky had brought the planet Venus into view, which lay shimmering on the horizon. Clouds were whispers of cotton in the wind and the dying sunset had painted their bottoms a dusky rose. Such sights had always moved Zac in the past, yet now they only served to tell him he was racing time.

Talbot put slack in the sails as they rounded Moro Rock, and Zac strained to see if he could make out the masts of a vessel still at anchor there. He was working on a cord and fashioning a strap for his shotgun. *Perhaps I've been wrong,* he thought. *Maybe going to Cambria first to get one of Talbot's boats was a mistake.* He knew he had to play for time and cause Hogan's ship to miss the tide if he could, yet maybe he'd miscalculated.

There it was! Across the narrow bar, Zac could see the masts of the tall ship. Men seemed to be in the rigging and there were lights in the cabin.

"Stay right here in the middle of the channel, Race. Drop your sails and your anchor."

"What do you have in mind, laddie? Do you want me to slip you ashore?"

Zac made no reply as Talbot dropped the sails; he merely worked at fashioning the charges he'd taken from the man's shelf in Cambria. He had bound them together with cord and fixed the fuses to blow simultaneously. Finishing the charge, he took out his pipe and decided on a last smoke while he could be sure of dry matches and tobacco. Carefully, he packed the briar, and lit a match. He touched it to the tobacco.

"It's time for a swim, Talbot."

"What?" The man seemed puzzled.

"You and I are going for a little swim tonight, only you are swimming for the sandbar out there and I'm about to make for the ship."

"Why? I don't understand."

"Oh, it'll be much clearer in about five minutes."

"What about my boat? Who'll handle her?"

"Your boat, my businessman friend, is going for a little swim too." Zac pointed the shotgun in Talbot's direction and motioned toward the side. "I'd suggest you get on with your paddling."

With that, Zac poked the end of the fuses into his pipe bowl and drew on the pipe, watching the sparks fly off the end of his nose. He smiled at Talbot, took a last puff on the tobacco, and rolled the smoking makeshift bomb into the open cockpit leading to the bottom of the boat. Then he slung the shotgun over his shoulder, stuffed the pipe into his jeans, and jumped overboard feet first into the cold harbor.

The waters were bracing. The day had been hot and the grass fire and warm offshore winds served to make the cold Pacific harbor seem even more shocking to Zac's system. Still, it had a numbing effect on his shoulder. He looked back to see Talbot splashing in the opposite direction and heard the muffled roar of the charges in the bottom of the fishing boat. They had been small explosives, designed to hurl a harpoon into the back of a whale, but combined, he felt sure they would puncture the hull of such a small boat.

"Boom . . . boom . . . boom." Loud rapid-fire explosions ripped through the still night air. Flames erupted on the small vessel and Zac could see it start to settle in the channel. He swam away from the direct line of sight leading from the clipper ship to the small burning boat. The last thing he wanted was a rescue. If he could get aboard while the crew was distracted by watching his handiwork, he'd more than accomplish his objective, and with any luck at all the channel exit would be blocked and need to be cleared by larger charges. He listened to the shouts of the crew members and the loud orders to the rigging. They were tying back the canvas.

Zac struggled in the cold water aft of the ship and slapped against the side of the hull. He could clearly see the name of the vessel in the shimmering moonlight off the cold water. It was the *Blue Goose*. There was something else, however. Underneath the word *Goose* were faint letters that had been painted over. It was certain that few people had the opportunity of seeing the name of Hogan's ship from the uncomfortable vantage point in which Zac Cobb now found himself.

He reached into his belt and took out his knife. Scraping beneath the O's in the ship's name, he could distinguish a W and an A. *Swan,* he thought. *This is the* Blue Swan, *not the* Blue Goose.

He was attempting to scrape the area around

235

the G, in order to expose the S, when the knife slipped from his fingers and into the murky water. He knew the chill was getting to him. Now with no knife and wet guns, he'd be in bad shape. He knew the odds of a misfire were something he couldn't rely on; he'd be defenseless.

He moved around the ship and quickly found a rope ladder with several longboats tied up and bobbing near it. The ladder was on the shore side of the vessel, however, and away from the fire and the sinking smaller boat. Counting on the crew being distracted, he began the ascent up the ladder. Talbot had been right. The swim had strained his shoulder, and now the excruciatingly painful climb up the ladder was unbearable. Glancing down at the bandages, he could see he'd sprung another leak. Blood was trickling down his chest.

He peered over the rail and saw the silhouettes of the crew on the opposite side of the ship. They were staring at the fiery fishing boat now settling into the channel. He swung his foot over the side of the rail. Water dripped off his clothing — water mixed with blood.

He moved silently to the open cargo hold and scampered down the ladder to the lantern-lit space below. Crouching beside the ladder, Zac could see it was empty, but around the walls of the hold he could see benches, sleeping platforms, and large casks where fresh water was kept.

His grandfather had told him about the horrible slave ships he'd seen as a boy. Zac himself had watched slave auctions in town before the war, and now he felt that what he was in to was a sinister look back in to history. The only thing missing were the leg-irons. Yet, in a darkened corner there *was* something. It was a man. A man lying on a sleeping platform, chained to the wall!

Zac stood erect and moved toward the figure, who could now clearly see him. Although still in the shadows, the man sat upright and lifted his feet off the deck, pressing his back to the bulkhead wall. "Pleese, no harm me. I already tell you what I know."

"I mean you no harm," Zac said. "Who are you, and what are you doing down here?"

"I am Me Low. I work for the railroad and I very sorry. I try to tell them about the opium coming in the whale oil. I find out. I tell. But they still no let me go." The man began to cry in the dark and wring his hands as well as his body into contorted motions. "Is my sister all right?" he asked.

"Who the blazes is your sister?" Zac asked.

"Oh, she nice girl. She work for Missy Hays in cafe. They tell me if I not help them find how the Tong is bringing its opium in, they going to kill her. They make me be spy. Is she all right?"

"I know nothing about your sister, but I am looking for Miss Hays. How did you get here?"

"The railroad, I tell them what I know about the Tong supply; they try to take it, but two men killed. They think I betrayed them so they bring me here. I think they take me back to China and sell me as slave. They bring many Chinese here on this boat to work for railroad; now they take me back. I no know what to do. Pleese, help me."

Half to himself Zac said, "It seems I can't turn around without finding another helpless person who's in trouble because of something I've done."

Louder, he said, "Look, whoever you are, I don't know what I can do for you, fella; frankly, I'm not even sure I can get myself out of here, but I'll do what I can." Zac took the soaked shotgun from around his shoulder and unbuckled his gun belt. "Here, stick this hog-leg some-where." He took the pistol and shoved it into his belt. "Hang on to this gun belt too. No matter what happens, it ain't gonna get much worse for you down here."

Zac moved off down the dark corridor, leaving the softly lit room. Inching his way through the darkness, he could see light under many of the doors he passed. He was certain now, deep in his soul, that behind one of these rooms, Jenny was being kept as a prisoner. The problem was, which one.

Then he saw it! It was a door unlike all the others, a door with a sliding outside lock. He held his ear to the door, listening to the silence on the other side, hoping for any sound that might tell him it was Jenny's room. He had placed his hand on the lock and started to slide it forward when he heard footsteps and voices coming down the stairs. It was Hogan's voice!

"Blast it all! We've got to clear that channel

tonight and sail within the next two hours, do you hear me? If we're not underway by then, all may be lost. I thought those men were supposed to be the best, to be competent. Now, we're running like rats."

"Captain, it was truly uncanny. T'was the most amazing thing I've ever seen in all me born days. I swear by all the saints I thought we had them dead to rights, then that old man showed up."

He stroked his flaming red beard. "Now, Cap'n, sir, we didn't 'zackly go and check the hill; that old man's Spencer moved us out right quick. I'm plenty sure, though, the fire burned them good. If it did, we've got little to fret ourselves about."

Zac recognized the voice of the man who was with the captain, but Hogan was blocking his view of the man's face. He had taken several steps back into the darkened passageway and remained in the shadows. He could see Hogan shake his head.

"I've got to worry. If we're discovered, it'll be my neck that's stretched. I'll feel a lot safer when we're out on open sea."

The man hidden from view broke in, "And a lot more amorous, I'll wager."

Zac could see that Hogan's companion was doing his best to put the captain's mind at ease and allow him to forget about his failure on the road.

Recovering his train of thought, Hogan barked out orders, "Have some men take two of those longboats out there and load them with dynamite.

We'll blow that scow out of the water if necessary."

Zac saw Hogan step aside and there he was, the man with the red beard! It was all he could do to restrain himself in the dark.

"Fitz, maybe keeping that Chinaman back there is a bad idea," Hogan contemplated. "I think when we clear the channel, we should feed him to the fish."

Zac saw the redbeard look down the dark passageway. He knew if either of the men decided to walk to the hold where the man was imprisoned, they would run right in to him in the hallway. He had to find a place to hide. He wasn't there to fight, he only wanted to free Jenny. Carefully, he inched his feet backward.

"Skipper, I'm a not liking it with that woman on board, either. There's little blame that can be laid on us for making money at the expense of the Chinese, but kidnapping a white woman is another matter."

"You worry too much about her. She'll be my wife or she'll fetch a good price in Shanghai. Besides, if those railroad men you went with had gotten their job done, our worries would be over."

Zac's next step backward met with a smack in to a bucket. It moved across the floor, reverberating down the passageway. "Who's there?" Hogan shouted.

"That be no rat," the redbeard said. In a lower voice he added, "Cap'n, if'n ye stay here in the light, I'll be goin' up top and around. I'll bring a candle and we'll have a look-see."

Zac backed down the black passageway and could see Hogan continue to peer into the darkened corridor. He knew he had to reach the hold before the redbeard got around there with a light.

When he reached the twilight-filled space, he could see the bright light and the legs of men coming down the ladder. Quickly, he glanced around the room and moved without hesitation to one of the large oak water kegs. He stepped into the cold, fresh water, sloshing some of it onto the floor and, settling into the barrel, lowered the lid into position.

"Bring those lights down here."

Zac recognized the voice of the redbeard.

"Let's move down the gangway now and look alive. If this be who I think it is, we've got some scores to settle tonight."

Zac only hoped the Chinaman on the cot would silently keep what he'd seen to himself. When Zac had talked to him, however, the man had seemed desperate enough to say anything to save his skin. With new light brought into the hold now, he also hoped the shotgun and the gun belt he had left with the man were still well concealed.

"Here, look at this." Zac could clearly hear the voices down the passageway. "There's water on the floor, and blood!"

Zac's nose bobbed above the water line in the oak barrel and he could see the brighter light passing his position. He waited for the inevitable questioning of the Chinaman on the cot, but all was silent. Zac wondered if the crew thought the man asleep, or dead. He listened to the red-bearded mate bark out orders to the men who had descended into the hold with him.

"You three, move on down the gangway. Check all the doors, very careful now. Look lively, we can't let this one escape, not this time, not now."

The sounds of the crew grew more muffled, and Zac strained to hear as they moved through the ship, checking each lock and each door.

He intensified his efforts at remaining quiet inside the huge freshwater cask. It wasn't easy. His bobbing head pressed his nose against the lid and it was a struggle to keep still in the cold, crouched position.

The sounds of the crew had grown more distant, but Zac felt no safer. He noticed that the bright light that had filled the hold now seeped through the cracks in the barrel. He wasn't sure if the light had been placed in some strategic spot in the large room and abandoned, or if it were still being held by the silent first mate; but from where he waited in his watery grave, he sensed the mate's eyes on his hidden position. He was almost afraid to breath as his head pressed in to the oak lid.

Then in a split second the lid was off and light flooded the barrel. He was exposed, and staring into the eyes of the red-bearded first mate. Before he could think the mate's knife took a downward plunge into the water, seeking its target.

With his left hand, Zac painfully reached up

and took hold of the sailor's arm, guiding it down past him. Then rising from the cask in a rush of water, he grabbed the man's belt with his right hand and pulled him down into the barrel.

Driving the redbeard hard to the bottom of the cask, Zac dropped his knees into the man's chest, pinning him under the water. Zac maintained his grip on the knife as the man thrashed around, sending water splashing over the edge onto the now-darkened floor.

Gurgling screams of the struggling mate echoed in the tight oak chamber, and the candle wick sizzled as it rolled through the growing puddle of drinking water on the floor. Beneath his weight, Zac could feel the man's hands clawing for leverage in a desperate struggle for survival. *Not this time,* Zac thought. *I've let you go too many times. You'll stay where you are!*

Zac looked toward the gangway in the direction of the search party, but could only see open doorways with light streaming from them, accompanied by muted talk. He held tightly to the man's legs and to the knife, while his knees continued to hold the reluctant sailor to the bottom. In a short time, the man's muscles went slack and Zac stepped from the cask, carefully replacing the lid. His shoulder was now throbbing with pain, but, considering the alternative, he felt fortunate.

"Meester." Zac heard the small voice from the sleeping platform. He stepped toward the man, who was shaking on his cot. Zac realized that, in the dark, the Chinaman couldn't know which one had survived the fight. Still, Zac didn't trust him. He decided it was best to leave the prone and frightened man just exactly where he was. He wouldn't say a word.

The whisper turned more plaintive. "Meester, is that you? Meester?"

CHAPTER 21

Zac stepped into the dark corridor that formed the passageway from the hold to the forward compartments. The search party had vanished and all he could hear was the sound of men on the foredeck. Preparations were being made to get the ship under way, and he knew that the time he was living on was borrowed at best; there would be no third chance at finding Jenny. Quickly, he moved toward the door that had been bolted from the outside. Water dripped from his clothes, and he pushed back his hair as he pulled the lock forward. Cautiously, he slid the door open.

"Jen?" he called in a cautious whisper into the darkened room. "Jen, are you there?"

Suddenly a match ignited, and he saw Jenny, standing behind a bedside table. She touched the flame to the candle wick and stepped into the center of the room. As Zac closed the door, she rushed into his arms.

"Zac! Oh, Zac! I was beginning to give up hope." She looked up into his brown eyes and ran her hand through his wet hair. Their lips touched lightly, and then she held him at arm's length and looked into his eyes again. The candlelight reflected in them, and Jenny smiled. "I can't believe you're here." She kissed him again, this time with full abandon.

Zac had never felt such peace and comfort. It was his turn to look into her eyes, and he smiled warmly. "That was some kiss, Miss Hays. You been saving up?"

Before she could respond, his face turned serious. "I hate to break this up, but we've got to get off this ship. I don't know if we've got any help on the way, but we'd better be prepared to go it alone."

Jenny gasped as she saw Zac's shoulder for the first time. "You're bleeding! Here, let me help you." She sat him down on the bed and in the flickering candlelight she lit several lamps that hung from the beams. "The captain gave me a needle and thread to sew my dress. It looks like your shoulder needs the stitches more."

Too weak and exhausted to protest, Zac allowed Jenny to thread the large needle and begin the arduous task of forming a suture on the open wound. She plunged the needle deeply into the inner tissue, and Zac winced in pain. After several awkward attempts, Jenny managed to close the gaping flesh.

Leaning her head toward him, she pressed her mouth against his chest and snapped the thread with her teeth, then collapsed next to him on the bed. Zac reached over and took the candle off the bedside table. Holding the flame to the closed wound, he grimaced as the melting wax cauterized the edges. Replacing the candle in its stand, he reached out to her with his good arm, slowly caressing her hair. "I didn't realize how handy you were," he said softly.

She shook her head and answered, "I could think of a more romantic thing to say, Zachary Cobb."

"I'm sorry, Jen. Being handy is a high compliment where I come from."

Zac was looking into her blue eyes and leaning forward for another kiss when the door to the room harshly slid open.

Standing in the doorway was Captain Michael Hogan. His white shirt was open and he held a gleaming cutlass. Through his large black beard, he grinned with a look of satisfaction.

Zac's hand dropped to his belt to pull his revolver, but he quickly realized it was gone.

"Well, Mr. Cobb, we meet at last, and I have the pleasure of having you aboard my ship." Jenny rose and silently slipped away from the bed as Zac got to his feet.

The smiling sailor brandished a wide smile, which Zac quickly erased. "*Your* ship, Captain? I managed to get a good look at the name of this vessel while climbing aboard. You may call it the *Blue Goose*, but its original name was the *Blue Swan*. I think the authorities will be very interested in examining your papers."

Jenny moved toward the captain, keeping the bedside table between them. "You weren't Henry's friend at all," she said slowly. "You're his murderer, a pirate, and a thief!"

"Harsh words, my dear, for your future husband."

Zac reached to his waist, without taking his eyes off the captain, and unbuckled his large leather belt. The movement caught the sailor's eye and he let out a laugh.

"Do you think I'll let you give me a whipping with that belt of yours, Cobb?"

Zac wound the end of the belt around his right fist. He let the silver buckle dangle beside his leg.

Seeing the buckle, the captain held up his cutlass to the light. "This blade of mine will cut you to ribbons. Then I'll take what's left of you and feed it to the sharks!"

Jenny circled to the left and raised her voice in desperation. "You are a man of no moral value, Michael Hogan. Have you no decency? Lies, lies, lies — your whole life is a lie, a sham and a lie!"

The captain's reply was cool and calm. It oozed from his lips like a deadly serpent from its hole. "My life is dedicated to profit, my dear. The trade of Chinese labor and other commodities is — shall we say — very profitable? Your Henry wanted no part of it. He was *above* it all, so I simply poisoned him." Jenny gasped. A sickening smile crossed the captain's face, and he said matter-of-factly, "Then I took the *Blue Swan*. Ships such as this one deserve to make a large profit. I will continue to see that it does."

Jenny stepped forward and registered a hard slap on the captain's cheek. The two stood in the candlelight exchanging penetrating stares of disdain. The man's face took on a rosy hue, but he remained calm. Then, smiling, he said, "You will pay for that, Jennifer, my dear. I like a woman with spirit. It makes their ultimate humility all the more satisfying. But, meanwhile, I have the distinct pleasure of killing someone else you love."

"Jen, step away," Zac commanded. "Let me deal with the man. Hogan, you're a coward. You poisoned a man who was your shipmate, and you've demonstrated a cunning ability to hire killers to do your dirty work for you. Now, let's see how you face up to a man who knows what you are."

The captain moved toward the center of the room and circled his sword in Zac's direction. Zac stepped forward and swung the belt over his head. The buckle flashed in the candlelight.

"Don't be looking for any help from town, Cobb." The sailor smiled and continued to circle the point of his sword. "I have a man who's taking care of that sheriff friend of yours, a man who doesn't like to fail. In a few minutes my crew will blast that wreck you used to bottle us up, and we'll be heading out to sea. Your woman will belong to me and your body will belong to the fish."

The cutlass swung out at Zac, but the agent's head darted backward and he slung the belt at the captain. The silver buckle stung the man's wrist, but he held the sword steadily.

The clash of the two men was interrupted by

an explosion on the water. From the porthole on the bulkhead wall, a flash could be clearly seen. "That would be my crew blowing up the derelict you so conveniently sank for us. We ought to be underway fairly soon, minus you, of course" — the captain brandished the sword at Zac's head — "and far ahead of any help that might be coming from town."

Zac returned the captain's smile. "I hope you're not looking for any help from that Irish mate of yours, Captain. I left him at the bottom of one of your freshwater barrels. He's had all the drink he cares to have." With that, the sailor lunged forward and the point of his sword nicked Zac's right arm.

Zac grabbed the captain's arm and the two men wrestled for control of the blade. Hogan swung his arms up and held the blade high as they struggled.

On any other occasion, Zac's strength would have been more than a match for his opponent, but the shoulder wound had weakened him and wrestling with both arms above his head was both painful and exhausting.

The floor was slippery with the water Zac had brought in on his clothes, and now it came back to haunt him. In the struggle with the captain, Zac's foot slipped, causing him to loose his grip on his healthy opponent. Down came the hilt of the cutlass on the top of Zac's head. The blow staggered him. Hogan brought down the butt of the sword again. The second blow shattered the agent's consciousness and left him in a pile at Hogan's feet.

Jenny screamed, "Don't! Please, stop! I'll give you whatever you want; just leave him alone."

Hogan smiled. "Jenny, my dear, you'll give me whatever I want in any case."

Suddenly Jenny spotted Tiataglo at the open door. He stood with his legs apart, armed with a harpoon.

"Stop him, Tiataglo! For God's sake, stop him!"

Hogan whirled to face his unexpected adversary. "What are you doing here, you monkey? Don't make a fool of yourself. Get up those stairs and make preparations for sailing."

The islander shook his head. "No, my Captain, I won't do that. What you do is a wicked thing. This lady is my friend. You must let her go."

The captain lowered his sword and stepped toward his muscular opponent. He smiled and lowered his voice. "Now old friend, this is business. We can't let our personal feelings get in the way, can we?"

Jenny watched in horror as the captain's smooth voice seemed to hold his would-be adversary spellbound, like a snake charming a small bird. Then Zac stirred at her feet, and Hogan swung his head around to make sure the agent was still on the floor. He turned back to the open door and held out his left hand to the dark-skinned sailor. "I'm going to need your help, my friend."

With those deceitful words, the captain thrust his cutlass forward like the tongue of a poisonous serpent and penetrated the ribs of the whaler with a sudden and swift motion.

Ugh. Jenny saw the utter surprise written on her friend's face. His eyes widened and his lips moved as if to speak, but he silently sank to the floor, holding the harpoon up in the direction of his assailant, with no power to use it.

The captain reached around the protruding harpoon tip and pulled the sword from the chest of the dark-skinned man as blood gushed from his body. The seaman's eyes were wide open, still in a state of shock and surprise.

Hogan took off the sash from around his own waist and wiped the blood from his blade. Staring into Tiatagalo's confused eyes, the captain offered the dying man a final explanation, "Business is business, old friend, and nobody stops me from doing what is necessary to maintain that business."

Zac raised his head and looked through the blur to see the captain turn around, his face bathed in an expression of evil victory. One glance at Jenny, though, and the captain's smile was gone. She had seized the glass of brandy and hurled the lukewarm liquid into his face. It burned his eyes and soaked his beard. Without a second's hesitation, she grabbed the flickering candle and shoved it into the burly man's face, igniting his beard with a flame that spread over his entire face.

He screamed in horror and stumbled backward,

dropping his sword as he sought to beat out the flames. As the two watched in disbelief, he slipped on the wet planking and crashed to the floor on top of the islander's still extended harpoon. When he came to rest in the dying man's arms, the deadly tip of the weapon protruded six inches out from the captain's breastbone.

On the foredeck of the vessel, Zac and Jenny stood watching the road as Bridger rode up with the posse. The moon hung low and the night stars filled the heavens, forming an outline against the dark, massive shape that was Moro Rock.

As the sheriff dismounted in the distance, Zac said to Jenny, "I've never been more happy to see that big hombre."

Jenny wrapped her arms more tightly around him.

"Why, do people feel so much at home in chains?" Zac asked. He had freed the Chinaman in the hold below, and had told Jenny of his innocent errand — one that had turned a simple favor into a nightmare for the two of them.

"What do you mean?" Jenny questioned Zac.

He stared at the sky a moment, then looked down toward the open hatch cover. "That Chinaman. He's still sitting next to his chains, like he doesn't want to leave them. I gave him my shotgun earlier tonight and he's still sitting there in shock. I don't get it."

Jenny looked up into Zac's eyes as something dawned on his consciousness.

"It's strange," he said, "but I guess I'm not much different. I've been in chains for years, but today something snapped." He looked at Jenny and his eyes misted over. "I just witnessed two people give up their lives for someone else, and they weren't even family. I've seen it happen in wartime, but this was different. Francisco tried to help me and died for it, and that islander down there tried to defend you and lost his life."

Looking up at the stars shimmering on Moro Bay he said, "I suppose I've been away from my roots too long. I've gotten hard, and forgotten what love looks like. You know, you can't really live for something, Jenny," he said, turning toward her again, "until you're ready to die for it."

Instinctively, he patted his pockets. His pipe was gone, but he continued, "I know I am loved, Jenny. I know a little boy that needs me, and I know you love me, and maybe you need me too. I just don't know where to go from here. See, I've always figured I'm the kind of man that's meant to be alone, someone who needs nobody and is needed by no one. I'm just not sure how to change what I am." He paused and looked down the darkened ship's hold. "I guess all of us feel more at home in the chains we're used to wearing."

Bridger's longboat finally reached the ship and he climbed aboard with several of the posse members.

Zac greeted him. "We heard you were dead."

"Not hardly. Though it wasn't much my do-ing."

Bridger paused to take a long look at Jenny. "It's mighty good to see you, girl. We were all worried sick about you."

He nodded toward Zac. "This fella here — I've never seen a man more driven than he was to-day."

Then to Zac he said, "I put that railroad su-perintendent under arrest. He seemed surprised to see me again. 'Course, he won't be in jail long. If a jury finds him guilty I'll have to go after everyone in the state from the Governor on down. He's just a man that works for that whole bunch up there, and they do take care of their own."

After rowing back to shore, Zac found the buckboard with Hans in it and a sleeping Skip in the back. He turned to Jenny and took her hand. "That little fella back there has gone a long way to making me feel human again. He gave me someone to look after and protect. Kind of a good feeling."

"Who is he?" she asked.

"It's a long story. But he's going to be a part of my life from here on out."

The employees of G.K. Hall hope you have enjoyed this Large Print book. All our Large Print titles are designed for easy reading, and all our books are made to last. Other G.K. Hall books are available at your library, through selected bookstores, or directly from us.

For information about titles, please call:

(800) 223-2336

To share your comments, please write:

Publisher
G.K. Hall & Co.
P.O. Box 159
Thorndike, ME 04986